STAGECOACH TO OBLIVION

ALSO BY JARRET KEENE

Kid Crimson Westerns

Gunpowder Mountain

The Guns of Goblin Valley

PRAISE FOR GUNPOWDER MOUNTAIN

"[Keene] is one hell of a writer."

— PETER BRANDVOLD, AUTHOR OF THE
SHERIFF BEN STILLMAN SERIES

"Packed with gritty action, *Gunpowder Mountain* is a pulse-pounding potboiler that also happens to be a very fine novel. Keene's taut and gutsy prose at once honors and renews the conventions of the Western genre, bringing to mind masters like Elmore Leonard, John Jakes and Walter Van Tilburg Clark. Sustained excellence from cover to cover."

— STEPHEN B. ARMSTRONG, AUTHOR
OF *I WANT YOU AROUND: THE RAMONES
AND THE MAKING OF ROCK 'N' ROLL HIGH
SCHOOL*

"Keene is a masterful writer of dialog and a superb weaver of tales crafted, I am convinced, with a slight smirk on his face. Gunpowder is rich in authentic and impressive detail, a product of the author's steadfast penchant for research."

— STEVE BORNHOFT, PROFESSOR,
JOURNALIST, COMMUNICATION
PROFESSIONAL

STAGECOACH TO OBLIVION

A KID CRIMSON WESTERN
BOOK 3

JARRET KEENE

WOLFPACK
PUBLISHING
— EST 2013 —

Stagecoach to Oblivion
Paperback Edition
Copyright © 2024 Jarret Keene

Wolfpack Publishing
1707 E. Diana Street
Tampa FL 33610

wolfpackpublishing.com

Paperback ISBN 978-1-63977-534-7
eBook ISBN 978-1-63977-617-7
LCCN: 2024944743

Cover Illustration by Claudio Bergamin

for Dick Ayers (1924-2014)

STAGECOACH TO OBLIVION

1

THE STAGE DRIVER STOOD ACE-HIGH IN Virginia City. The image of a man perched atop a Concord, cracking his long whip above a six-horse team, stirred the hearts of residents in our mining town. It was an occupation that tickled the national fancy too, especially female readers of slick East Coast magazines and the adolescent audience for puerile dime novels. During the War between the States, stage drivers cemented their status as popular heroes. After all, they were brave enough to risk frequent stoppages by bandits who emerged from the sage to get the drop on them. You needed a spine of steel to haul passengers across a savage landscape and no one was steelier than my buddy Hank Monk. He deserved all the respect and praise that was due.

Hank, the Man in the Harness, kept civilization in Virginia City intact with endless stagecoach deliveries, shipping gold bullion, opera singers, and bank magnates from California to Nevada and back again. No one matched Hank's speed, reliability, and dexterity. He was also a talker, brimming with tales of madcappery up and down the trails of the West. We made an effective team. When I worked alongside him, clutching at the ready my cutdown shotgun—a brass-barreled smoothbore flintlock —he couldn't fail.

One time though, we came close to falling short of success.

Ralston was the town railroad director, tasked by Orion Clemens, Secretary of the Nevada Territory, to expand the line from Reno to Virginia City. I did jobs for Ralston as a way of saving money to buy a citrus farm in California before I ended up dead on account of my profession. Riding shotgun with Hank was a lucrative job. It *needed* to pay well, since I was married now, and the sooner I made the nut for our farmland, the faster my pregnant Poppy and our adopted urchins Ezra and Sarah and I could leave Virginia City. Hank and I had just delivered a gaggle of mining executives to Placerville, and were returning with passengers from San Francisco, when we approached the station at Cisco station. We topped a rise thick with desert pines and looked down on the glorified eatery and the creek beyond it. As we came out of the trees and started down the mesquite-lined hillside, Hank and I shared a look.

The station seemed abandoned. No cooking smoke. No sign of the manager, Wallace, or his sons, Rusty and Calvin, who typically pitched horseshoes or tanned leather or scrubbed the outhouse this time of day. The kitchen door swung in the breeze, clapping against the wooden structure.

"Dang, where *is* everyone?" Hank wondered, leaning back with the reins held high and pushing his boot against the brake lever. "Sabrina always has clothes drying on the line."

"Maybe she has the day off," I said. "Took the boys to see her mother in Kingvale."

"Come on, Kid. This here Concord we're riding squeals like an abolitionist in a West Virginia engine house. We made enough noise to get *some*one's attention."

We sat there listening to the eerie silence for a moment.

The woman we were ferrying finally spoke up. "Driver, can I please step outside this carriage? I've grown peckish and my limbs ache from disuse."

"Yes, I could use a sandwich and a stretch," the young man said, no relation to the woman. His voice was somehow more feminine than hers. His long hair and undersized hat indicated—to me, anyway—that he was minimally skilled and of limited value. Another soft-handed soul destined for vagrancy and an early death.

"You might have to wait for us to reach Virginia City," I told the effete boy.

Hank sighed. "Think they're butchering a hog behind the shed for tomorrow morning's bacon?"

I shrugged. "Only one way to find out."

Holding the sawed-off scattergun under my armpit, I climbed down. I was eager to keep going, yet the thought of eating nothing but trail dust for the next several hours was demoralizing. Also, I was suddenly uneasy about my friends here at the station.

"Kid," Hank said, remaining in the buckboard. "Let *me* take a look. I'm old and your life is just beginning, what with you being a new husband with a baby on the way."

I laughed, keeping my eyes focused on the station, gun at the ready. "Hank, just because I'm married doesn't make me any less lethal."

"Oh, I know that. It's just that you have more to lose now, with Poppy all hung up on you."

"The world takes everything away," I said, lowering my voice so only he could hear me. "Now pick up your Henry rifle and train it on the outhouse."

"Sure, Kid." He aimed his gun at the reeking privy. "Someone preparing to snipe in there, you think? Could be one of Wallace's boys having trouble. You know how young'uns today love to eat borderline garbage as long as it's thoroughly salted and sugared."

"We're about to find out." My boots crunched on the gravel path leading to the porch.

"Kid, if everything's okay and nothing's on the stove, can you ask Sabrina for some of her cold cornbread? Wallace's wife is an unrivaled baker, I tell you."

I didn't respond. Instead, I called out the station manager's name: "Wallace! Overland Stage is here with hungry passengers!"

Our ears pricked up at the distracting noise of a boot scraping the wooden floor of the station and soon a man —skinny, bearded, dust-ravaged—was standing in the open doorway, his Schofield leveled at me. In the moment, I realized he'd made the sound to signal his accomplice in the crapper.

"Hit 'em, Hank!" I yelled, dropping to the ground as the man at the door fired a shot that sent my black flat-brimmed hat flying off my skull. Hank and I blasted our guns simultaneously, my shot missing yet splintering the door frame, causing my target to retreat back into the station.

I sprang up and got enough momentum to leap onto

the porch. Lowering my shoulder, I rammed the door as it started to swing shut. Already cracked from use, it broke into three pieces as I tumble-rolled into the main room and saw the man with the Schofield flipping a table for cover.

He got it over in time to deflect my second blast, but because I'd sawn down the barrel, he ended up getting buckshot-nicked. He fell to his knees, his gunless hand pressed against his bloody neck. "Bastard!" he screamed.

"Been called worse," I admitted.

My enemy didn't roll over. Raising his Schofield again, he managed a wild shot that ricocheted off an iron pot hanging from the ceiling, a bullet whizzing past my ear. I cut the distance between us, kicking him to the ground and using my gun to pin his shooting wrist to the floor, the hot metal of my muzzle on his skin. He released the pistol in the hope that I'd withdraw the burning barrel.

I didn't and he screamed. "*Worst* kind of bastard!"

"How many?" I pushed harder on his hand.

"Gah!" he screeched. "Me and Joaquin is all, I swear!"

I stomped his groin to let him know he'd be held to his promise. "There's only *you*, because Hank never misses. Where's Wallace?"

"In the livery with his family," he whimpered, voice higher now and strained, the smell of burning flesh turning the air acrid. "We had nothing to do with it!"

"Keep talking," I said, agitated from the revelation that Wallace's family had been slaughtered.

"My name's Gentry. We showed up here after selling whiskey to the Indians on the way back from Pinto Creek."

"Where's your wagon?"

"Burned to ash. Along with the other five members of

our gang. Had the misfortune of running into the Anni-hilators. Probably stopped through here before finding us."

The mention of this outfit chilled my blood. The Annihilators were a renowned trio of pitiless bounty hunters that caused mayhem in Texas years earlier. They'd been secretly hired by Texas Governor Lubbock to round up forty-one suspected Unionists, resulting in the Great Hanging at Gainesville. A gruesome chapter of a war that my sources suggested would end any day now. Me, I wasn't sure that enough blood could be spilled to satiate the death machine Lincoln had unleashed across this nation, from Richmond, Virginia, to Virginia City, Nevada.

A sound from the porch caused me to pivot. Still pinning Gentry's arm, I leveled my Colt. The man I suspected to be Joaquin nursed his shoulder as Hank prodded him into the station with the barrel of his rifle. "Look what I found."

"Latrine viper," I said. "Your aim's getting bad."

"Nah, I meant to chip him. This one ain't old enough to have a single scrotum hair."

Joaquin was indeed baby-faced, but he wasn't bashful. "You don't scare me, Kid Crimson. I'll fight you bare-handed any day and whup you good."

I reached down to grab Gentry by the collar, dragging him like a sack of potatoes to a table. "Sit up."

Hank shoved Joaquin toward the same bench. "We need an explanation, tadpole."

"I'm bleeding bad," Gentry said. "Can I just—"

"First," I cut him off, "tell me something. These Annihilators you claim torched your whiskey, what do they look like?"

"There's three of them. They're Texas boys with... well, they have unusual weapons."

"How so?" Hank said.

Gentry's voice grew hoarse. "One works a whip. Another shoots a coffee-mill gun. The third is the nastiest—he uses a pike to rip your head from your body. He did exactly that to our friend Barney."

"Pike?" Hank said.

"A long thrusting spear," I said.

"Yes," Gentry rasped. He needed medical attention and we were far from any doctor.

"He's bleeding bad," Joaquin said, glaring at me.

"I can see that. Who do they work for, these Annihilators?"

Gentry tried to speak, but nothing came out.

Joaquin spoke instead. "The devil himself. You better hope you don't run into them. We did and barely escaped with our lives."

"You ran into *us*," I said, "which is worse than anything on earth. That's why you're gashed."

Suddenly, the woman we were transporting stepped into the station. She appraised the situation, while—I could tell—searching for something edible. Her beauty made us all stare at her, even the bullet-scratched bandits. I quickly scanned her white-lace puff-sleeve blouse with lantern sleeves, plaid ankle-length skirt, and black leather half-boots. She wore glasses the way I'd never seen a woman wear them—with big frames that flattered her extraordinary hazel eyes instead of those tiny old maid suffragette spectacles that made men want to jump off a cliff. Her hair was vital and flowing, everything about her emanating youth and, yes, fertility.

"Ma'am," Hank said. "You might not want to witness these proceedings."

She shrugged. "I've seen bandits before." Her eyes landed on a bowl of apples and she reached for one. "Written about them plenty too." She took a bite and, pointing at pale Gentry, said through a mouthful, "The one that's neck-shot requires attention. I'll light the stove."

She set about doing exactly that as we observed her light the kindling with a match. She found a pitcher of water and poured it into a pot, then placed it on the metal plate. We all would've kept staring, but then Hank said, "Where's the other passenger, Miss, uh... Miss..."

"Dunn," she said, opening a leather satchel. "Clementine Dunn. Your male passenger—at least I *assume* he's male—refuses to leave the coach because of all the gunfire."

Her name sounded familiar, but I couldn't place it. "That looks like Hank's medicine bag."

"It is," Dunn said, handing me a small glass bottle and a cloth. "Carbolic acid. I'll give you the honor."

I took the bottle and poured some disinfectant into the cloth. "This will hurt."

Gentry nodded, then grimaced as the antiseptic did its work.

"Show me," Hank said to Joaquin. "We should bury poor Wallace and his family before they spoil."

After boiling a needle and thread, Dunn dragged a stool over to the bench and sat in front of Gentry, spreading her legs in a way that wasn't ladylike but made it easier for her to stitch the wound. She handed Gentry a whiskey bottle to numb the pain. He drank carefully, since swallowing was clearly painful. I observed, gun in hand.

"So you're a writer," I said to her, "who knows how to

patch up a whiskey trader. I don't know many scribes with such...multifaceted assets."

She paused to look at me, blowing a strand of hair away from her face. Then she resumed stitching. "You don't sound like a hired gun, Georgia. Were you educated out east?"

"Macon. My father owned a plantation."

"You had a tutor."

I nodded. "Straight from Paris."

Gentry unstiffened his body with relief as Dunn completed the stitch. He downed more liquor and slumped against the wall, exhausted. "Thank you, miss," he whispered.

She stood up to meet my gaze, using the rest of the hot water to scrub her hands. "You're an American killer who speaks French."

"And Latin. And Greek."

"Adonis in spurs."

"Venus *in sanguine*."

She reached toward me for what I imagined was an embrace, causing me to raise my arms clumsily. Instead, she plucked a chunk of cold cornbread from a ceramic plate and took a bite.

"I've written three full-length penny dreadfuls about you," she said, chewing inelegantly, yet hypnotically. "You're a hundred times more fascinating in the flesh than on the page."

Clementine Dunn. *That's* why the name rang familiar.

Standing in front of me was the author of the dime novels featuring stories based on my exploits in Virginia City.

"You've brought me a lot of unwanted attention," I said, "at a time when I need to disappear from the public imagination."

"I'm afraid that's not possible," she said. "Your books sell out on newsstands from San Francisco to Staten Island. I'm going to watch you in action and write down what I see...with a few embellishments."

I grabbed her arm as she was about to enjoy another bite of cornbread. I aimed to strongly discourage her literary plans when Hank and Joaquin returned.

"Kid," Hank said. "You need to see this."

2

INSIDE THE LIVERY, FLIES BUZZED AROUND THE corpses of Wallace and his family, a horrid scene that instantly scarred me, awakening the revengeful monster. I'd only chatted with Wallace and his family a handful of times in the last year, but I liked them and enjoyed their company. They'd fed me when I was hungry, and I'd envied the boys for their father who, as far as I knew, didn't pummel them on the regular. I remembered how the wife had smiled at her husband and sons. They seemed decent and kind, but now Confederate-licensed killers had executed them for no reason other than ghastly impulse. Bad men were going to die now no matter who they worked for.

"I don't need to see this, Hank," I said. "Give the boy a shovel and have him dig graves out behind the shed."

Joaquin gave me a mean look, but stayed silent.

"Not the bodies," Hank said. "Look at what someone scratched into the dirt there."

Shafts of light squeezed between wooden slats, illuminating what looked like the emblem of the Knights of the Golden Circle, a sinister and secret organization run by wealthy industrialists and sadistic plantation owners hellbent on establishing a slaveholding empire across the Americas and West Indies. The seal comprised a Greek cross with a star inside it, both symbols surrounded by a circle.

"These lunatics again," I said, recalling how, months earlier, the Knights had dispatched a Confederate commander and French nobleman, Prince Polignac, to Virginia City to extinguish our mining industry by means of giant guns. With the help of everyone in town, we foiled him, and Sarah, having befriended an escaped circus lion, turned Polignac into a snack for her big cat.

Hank had concerns. "Reckon these Annihilators are part of the conspiracy?"

I shrugged. "The Annihilators work for anyone who pays. Hell, they did jobs for the Union last year. They have no moral compass, unless you consider money a direction."

The heat and smell in the livery were getting to Hank. He removed his derby to wipe his forehead with his sleeve. "So the Knights recruit these Texas killers to, what, kill indiscriminately?"

"It's definitely a message they've sent," I said. "And I suspect they intended it for you and me."

"Well, can you translate? Killing Wallace and his wife and sons isn't just incomprehensible—it's pure evil."

Joaquin had had enough. "I need to—I should step outside for a moment."

Hank pulled a shovel off the nail it was hanging from and threw it at him. "Start digging with your good arm while you're out there. And let us know if you see them coming back."

Joaquin missed the catch, stooping to pick up the

tool. Bending over to retrieve it, he gagged from the wretched stink of the scene before us. Then he staggered into the yard.

As he did so, he nearly collided with the other passenger, who'd finally gotten up the gumption to leave the stage and join us. He absurdly tipped his hat to Joaquin, who ignored him to start stabbing dirt in the yard.

"Excuse me," the young man said, stepping into the shed. "But are we safe here?" Then the death smell hit him and he reached for a handkerchief as he retreated back into the sunlight. "Lord, preserve me!"

"Safer than in the coach," Hank said, walking outside with him. "What's your name again?"

"Eli Sackmary. Appraiser." He extended his hand to Hank but was rebuffed.

"What do you appraise, Sackmary?" I stepped from the shed to scan the horizon for dust clouds.

"Gold. Silver."

"You must be one of Ralston's," Hank said, clearing his phlegm and spitting. Hank had a beef with the Virginia City financier over a percentage he felt hadn't been honored. It was risky to haggle with Ralston, but Hank was too valuable to dismiss. Inevitably, Ralston would have to settle with the stage driver or confront the possibility of hiring someone untrustworthy and alcohol-prone to shuttle his administrants, foremen, and over-seers to and from California.

"I'm in his employ, yes," Sackmary said, handkerchief pressed to his nostrils, making his annoying voice even more grating. "I earned my degrees at the Mineralogy Academy in Zurich, Switzerland."

"Of course you did," Hank said. "What's your specialty?"

"Oversized, compact, waterworn masses of valuable minerals found in paleo-placer deposits."

"What's that mean?"

"Giant nuggets," I said.

Sackmary changed the subject, realizing he'd revealed too much. "What I said earlier about needing a sandwich? Never mind. I've lost my appetite."

"This route tends to have that effect," Hank said. "I'd be a fat man in most other lines of work."

"This route," I said, "is even more stomach-turning than usual. Pick up a shovel, Sackmary. You and I have digging to do."

"I—I don't think I've ever actually scooped a hole."

Hank appeared flummoxed. "You mean to say you're an expert mineralogist who's never dug a hole in the ground?" his voice rising in disbelief.

"I, well, sir—you know, I study the stones *after* they've been unearthed."

"Kid," Hank said, turning his attention. "What exactly are you and I transporting to Nevada?"

"The next generation," I confirmed. "The future of America."

"Is it just me? Or do they seem kind of soft."

"Speak for yourself," Dunn piped up, skirt bunched up, revealing muscular legs, one of which pushed on the lip of a shovel to help dig the graves. "I'm headed to Virginia City for the same reason as everyone else, including those ore-encrusted gunpowder-coated miners."

"What reason is that?" Sackmary asked.

"Hard currency."

The five of us kept digging into the late afternoon. We took breaks to care for the stagecoach horses and to feed and water Wallace's pigs. Finally, Joaquin and I dropped a body into each of the graves, poured lime on, and covered them with dirt. Afterward, we washed up, Hank heated up beans and coffee on the stove, and Dunn set the table inside the station house, placing a piece of poor Sabrina's delicious cornbread on each of the ceramic plates, including Joaquin's. No one ate too heartily, except for Dunn.

Sackmary fussily tucked a napkin into his collar. "Do you imagine they're looking for us?"

"The Annihilators?" Hank said.

"Who—who might they be?"

"The men responsible for killing the family," Dunn said flatly, slurping a spoonful of beans.

Sackmary put down his fork. "I meant the authorities. After all, we're well behind schedule."

"No one is searching," I said. "Ralston isn't worried."

"Why not?"

I didn't say anything.

Hank had enough of the quiet though. "Because the Kid is on this stage," he said.

"You're Kid *Crimson*? I've heard you're...unpredictable. Prone to violence."

"Don't believe everything you read in a dime novel," Dunn explained with a grin.

———

WE GAVE Joaquin and Gentry a couple of Wallace's horses, some water and cornbread, and sent them to Fort Churchill to report the atrocity at Cisco station. Whether they'd make it or not was anyone's guess, but I couldn't risk letting them travel with us for the short run to Virginia City. Joaquin was talking tough with me before he lit out, a clear indication he wasn't trustworthy. Moreover, because Hank and I hadn't seen the Annihilators with our own eyes, we couldn't be sure who'd killed Wallace and his family. I'd leave it for the US Army commander to sort out.

"Your whiskey days are done," I told Joaquin before he trotted away on a palomino. "If I catch you out here on the trail again, I'll shoot you dead."

He turned in his saddle to sneer his own threat. "You owe me a barehanded scrap, Kid." Then he turned his back to the setting sun and toward his own fate. I didn't envy him. I might've been a killer and a short-lived gun for hire, but I wasn't as dumb as a box of rocks and full of bravado to boot. I had a chance at least.

Before leaving, we affixed a wooden sign to the shattered entrance of the way station that read: ANNIHILATORS KILLED STATION OWNERS. LAST COACH—OVERLAND. We drove through the night, Hank burping and trumpeting from all the beans he'd eaten. There was enough space in the carriage for Dunn and Sackmary to lie down and steal some winks despite all the rocks and holes on the trail bouncing our wagon. The moon peeked from behind a cover of clouds, casting light and rough shadows on the trail, unsettling my nerves even further. The smell of pine was strong, the sound of the wind eerie. The cold grew biting and for a moment I considered grabbing a snooze inside the warmth of the coach. I thought about what Dunn might feel like with her gorgeous head on my chest. I also fantasized about yanking her out of the Concord and leaving her to her own fate, like Joaquin. In her effort to turn me into some kind of gunfighter-hero, she had put a target on my back. The most illiterate Virginia City riff-raff had started challenging me in the streets, having heard of my fictionalized reputation secondhand from kids like Ezra and

Sarah, who were being instructed in the new school-house by Bad Jace's lovely girlfriend, Lydia Sweet. Sweet had arrived from Oregon to bring reading, writing, and mathematical ability to our mining town.

Lydia's efforts worked, yes, but instead of doing Shakespeare-related homework, the kids were reading nonsense books written by the Clementine Dunns of the world. Instead of toiling under men like Ralston and John Mackay, the students learned arithmetic to perfect their business plans, such as overhead on Ezra's shoeshine stands. At least they were reading and doing multiplication and percentages, and the more I thought about it, the less I could really blame them.

Living in a mining boomtown rampant with noise and waste demanded escapism and money. I wanted my beautiful ragamuffins to win at the game of life, despite a stacked deck. I wanted my kids—including the one growing in Poppy's belly—to come of age without despising the world into which, without their say so, they'd been plunged. It had taken me years to come to terms with the abuse my father had inflicted, rage sharpening my heart to a knife's edge. On the plantation, I'd lost everyone who ever cared for me—my mother, my nanny, my lover. It was only when I met Poppy, who suffered her own losses in the British bombing of Canton during the Arrow War, that I learned how to love again, how to be vulnerable, kind, and affectionate. I wasn't cured by any stretch of the imagination. I still struggled to contain my wrath and adapt to a society that saw me as a tool to be used in case of emergency. Still, my perspective was improving.

Having my own family and an orchard in California was my chance to heal, to provide an example for our children to follow. No matter how hard circumstances pushed us, we could always push back. If people didn't like me because of something they read in a book or newspaper, that was fine. I'd be ready to meet them, to fight and defeat them, and so would my kids. I'd show them how. In return, they'd allow me to live on, to survive in a fashion I preferred—in their memories.

The rhythmic clomping of hooves nearly lulled me into dreamland. An owl hooted in a juniper that we passed and I watched Hank's head nodding, but never long enough for him to fall asleep. As we grew closer to Sun Mountain, I saw light guttering at the base, the pine forest slowly thinning as we reached the outskirts of town. We were at the part of the trail where the road turned narrow and treacherous, creating an otherworldly environment. I heard the faintest animal noise, like a lion growling, which caused Hank to shoot an uneasy glance in my direction.

Suddenly, the horses whinnied, quickly arresting our forward progress and causing Hank and I to grab hold of the rail under our seats to maintain our balance. Hank pulled the reins to calm the six-horse team, letting them know we had no desire to urge them forward. The Concord creaked to a standstill.

"Why did the horses stop, Kid?" Hank muttered, peering into the darkness. Our mouths opened in unison as we detected, fifty yards ahead, a pair of eyes reflecting the moonlight and the glow from our lantern. Then we heard a rumbling noise emanating from the murk, slowly padding toward us.

"Mountain lion," Hank hissed, raising his Henry rifle.

The creature was massive, tawny, stepping into the path, muscles rippling beneath its fur. Done growling, the lion gave a sudden roar that echoed through the canyon, freezing my spine.

I heard Clementine, inside the coach, say, "Is that what I think I heard?"

Sackmary whimpered a prayer, completely unready to defend himself.

"We need to frighten it away," Hank said, voice low and firm. He raised the barrel of his rifle to fire a warning shot into the air. The explosion reverberated like thunder, momentarily silencing the crickets. The horses, however, were bothered. Skittish from the blast and predator, they snorted and stomped their hooves, eager to get moving before the beast took a chunk out of their hides.

Unimpressed, the lion roared again, eyes fixed on us. I raised my shotgun and prepared to put it down, the tension palpable. But then in the lamplight I recognized a familiar mark on its face, a scar earned from the battle in Virginia City against Polignac's Confederate forces. I lowered my gun. "Hang on, Hank. I know this lion."

"Kid, you can't possibly—"

"C'mere, Uru. Good kitty. Still well trained, I see."

The big cat whined a bit as he headed for us.

"Sarah, you out there?!"

"Kid!" she called. "I'm here with Chaparral!"

Chaparral was my best friend and the piano player at the Blood Nugget, a whiskey-slinging tavern operated by Verbena, one of my employers and a woman I could never shake loose from my heart. Sure enough, Sarah and Chap, faces illuminated by carriage lanterns, approached in Poppy's two-horse buggy wagon.

Uru the lion sauntered up to our stagecoach, stood up on its hind legs to place its paws on my seat, and yawned. I rubbed his lower jaw, which he loved. Sitting next to me, Hank leaned away, his eyes wide and mouth hanging open. He'd driven hundreds of coach rides over the Sierra, but never experienced anything like this.

"Sarah wouldn't let us sleep, Kid," Chaparral said. "She made me come out here to find you."

"Perilous," I said, stroking the lion's thick mane. "Too many bandits at night."

"We had a contingency plan," a voice snarled. Bad Jace, my hulking ride-along buddy, emerged from the void, holding a Winchester atop an Appaloosa I'd given him as a gift for helping me save Virginia City a second time earlier in the year.

"Wow, everyone showed up looking for me," I said, restraining my emotion.

"We like you, Kid," Chap said, "even if you're a bit of a bugger at times."

The carriage door to the Concord opened. Not waiting to be helped down, Dunn climbed off the coach and walked over to greet my friends. "So these are Kid Crimson's accomplices. My name is Dunn."

No one said anything for a moment until Chap broke the silence. "Dunn? Not Clementine Dunn!"

"The very same," she said coyly.

"Fancy meeting you here. You're the one making the Kid out to be more than he is."

She smiled. "Kid Crimson will get exactly what's coming to him."

"What's that?" Bad Jace asked. "Civilization? Peace? Fatherhood?"

"Immortality," she said. Uru quietly pushed off from the wagon and walked over to the dime novelist, who didn't seem at all bothered by the presence of a jungle animal.

"That sounds like death." Bad Jace spat his chaw into the dust.

"The two," Dunn said, "are often blurred." She stoically extended her hand, which the lion met by nuzzling his whiskers against her fingers.

Sarah, the animal-wrangling girl, didn't seem pleased with this outcome.

"Is it safe to leave the stage now?"

Everyone looked at me with an expression of confusion.

"That's Sackmary. He's a gemologist."

"A *what* now?" Bad Jace wanted to know.

"He studies the products of the mining industry."

"In that case," Chaparral said, "he's an expert on the circles of hell."

"Let's show him every circle," I said. "Onward to Virginia City."

And off we went, another circus semi-parade—an actual African lion, a two-horse buggy with an eleven-year-old lion tamer and a saloon ivory tickler, a vicious killer on an Appaloosa who worshipped a schoolmarm, the big Concord with six mighty horses controlled by the West's greatest whip, an assayer who didn't know the working end of a shovel, and an immensely desirable novelist who was trying to get me killed. All we were missing was Hannibal, the armored elephant that helped win the Battle of Virginia City.

3

BESIDES MY ONGOING AND RIDICULOUS appearances in dime novels, there was another reason the bloom had fallen off my rose in Virginia City and it had to do with Sarah. Prior to her arrival, animal fighting had dominated local entertainment—dogfighting, cockfighting, even camel wrestling. Sarah's empathic bond with all creatures big and small made it impossible for her to ignore the cruelty that man inflicted. She was directly involved in ruining blood sport by showing up and, from the sidelines, influencing the beasts to inaction or to bite and lash at the hands of the owners as they attempted to stir their animals to violence. Eventually, the organizers of these events determined that her presence had a dampening effect and she was banned from attending. However, one particular exhibition nearly put me at the top of the vigilance committee's death list: the bear and bull showdown in the opera house.

Thanks to Lincoln's ceaseless war, there had been a lull, a revenue-killing dead patch, in scheduled performances in Virginia City. Desperate to pay off his construction debt, opera house director Myles Dominick allowed for a beer-spattered show pitting a 600-pound black bear against an intimidating Spanish matador-crushing bull. The event was packed, all 1,500 seats occupied by ornery miners and curious bankers and lawyers, even some of their wives. Sickened by so many uncultured mouth-breathers jamming the place, Chaparral left before the festivities got underway, leaving me, high up in the balcony, to absorb a harsh spectacle and to wait for someone I knew would have an effect on what transpired.

The bear initially cowered in the corner of the cage as the fierce bull charged, horns gouging, causing the bear to roar before clawing ineffectively. The bull dashed a second time with the same results, then a third. The bear lunged, gnashed, and scratched more vigorously, then headed back to his corner, waiting, lurking. The bull stood staring at his opponent, snorting aggressively, scratching his hooves on the heavy layer of sawdust that Dominick had poured onto the floor of the stage. Another attack on the bull's part crashed the bear against the cage's steel bars.

Having paid a dollar for admission, the crowd expressed dissatisfaction by smashing beer steins against the cage, broken glass mixing with the sawdust and cutting the bear's feet, causing blood to darken the floor. Drunken idiots attached a piece of red cloth to a curtain hook and waved it in the bear's face, urging him to charge the bull. It didn't work. Exhausted and battered, the bear lay flat on his stomach and chin, staring at the mob with hurt confusion in his eyes. This incensed the spectators, who began prodding him with broomsticks and whipping him with foils, tormenting him with their barbarism and clamor.

The bull didn't like this behavior either, slamming his horned noggin against the bars, creating a gap big enough for the bear to slip through. He quickly escaped the cage, standing upright and roaring like a bringer of death.

Sarah had crept into the opera house to join me in the balcony. We were appalled by what we witnessed. But that was nothing compared to what happened next.

Theatergoers screamed and stampeded. One of them drew a pistol and fired, missing the bear and causing a bullet to ricochet off the metal bars and graze a miner's thigh.

Dominick dimmed the structure's newfangled gaslights in an attempt to motivate patrons to exit the opera house. This, however, had the opposite effect, inciting people to toss their chairs at the bear, pacing the stage in angry confusion before leaping into the seats. At that same moment, the gaslights went out completely, immersing the opera house in darkness.

People desperately struck matches, yelling fiercely for the lights to be turned on. Disoriented and enraged, the bear mauled a banker to death, biting the man's face with gruesome ferocity, the screams of the dying financier muffled by the animal's lacerating maw. At this point, several theatergoers charged the bear with steak knives and assorted blades fastened to broom handles. But now the bull smashed his way out of the damaged cage and head-butted the young men, catapulting them into the air, their improvised weapons useless against such a powerful beast. Blood flew in all directions.

"Kid," Sarah said, looking up at me. "Let's help them."

"I'd rather not. They deserve a comeuppance."

"Not the men, the animals."

I grabbed her hand and we raced from the balcony down a side stairwell and into the swarmed lobby. It was a maelstrom of panicking knuckleheads. They collided with one another as they fled the building, one of them crashing into a mirror, the noise of exploding glass fraying everyone's nerves even further.

At that moment, pushing against the flow, Bad Jace—a notorious coyote-killer—and several tough guys arrived with rifles, eager to put down an animal that had eaten someone's face off. He saw me and didn't seem eager for a debate on the ethics of killing animals.

"Out of the way, Kid. We'll spare the bull, but the bear is due for a taxidermy appointment."

"You know better than to tell me to move, Bad Jace."

It was well known, especially to Bad Jace, that I didn't respond to false authority. I recognized none of the men he'd brought with him, my hand fluttering imperceptibly above my holstered gun.

Bad Jace sighed dramatically, so I knew what was coming. As the lobby emptied, he smiled, threw his rifle at one of his turd-faced buddies to catch, removed his jacket, and rolled up his sleeves. "Sarah, run along and tell Poppy to bring iodine for the Kid's busted mouth."

"I won't," she said, picking up a still-full popcorn bag someone had dropped on the fancy carpet on their way out. She perched herself on a staircase newel, snacking away. "Because that ain't how it'll happen, Bad Jace. Tell you what though, I'll fetch Dr. Scullard to amputate your arm after Crimson breaks it."

Bad Jace rolled his eyes and grunted with irritation before rushing me.

I moved aside and boot-swept his legs, sending him

crashing headlong into the concession area, his skull cracking open a beer keg, suds spewing everywhere, and foam drenching my eyes.

He recovered quickly, taking advantage of my burning vision to throw a haymaker that missed my chin but nearly shattered my collarbone. Then he swung a sharp wooden slat from the busted keg that sliced my forearm as I blocked it. I could feel wet blood oozing through my shirt.

I hadn't intended to defend animals from anyone's bullets, much less Bad Jace's. At the same time, it had been too long since the two of us had had a nasty punch-up, so now was as good a moment as any. He'd triggered the monster inside me and there was no retreat for either of us.

Bad Jace grabbed the slat with both hands, attempting to impale my damaged arm. I grabbed the cushion off a chair and blocked the razored wood, angling his follow-through momentum so that he was off balance. Then I boot-scraped his calf, eliciting a scream that made me smile. He tried to grab and clinch me up, but that was a tactic I'd been trained to deal with since I was nine years old, a pit-fighting boy in the Deep South. I let him get close enough to yank his arms toward me. Then I tumbled backward, using my legs to kick-boost him over and into the wall, smashing a gas lamp.

I sprung up from the floor, ready to uppercut him into an evening nap. Bad Jace, however, stumbled clumsily to his feet and, mistaking one of his buddies for me, took a wild swing and missed. Then he fell over, crashing into some furniture, and didn't get up.

"Kid," Sarah said, tossing a popcorn flake at me, which I caught in my mouth.

"Yum."

Bad Jace's three buddies came running at me, looking to clobber me senseless. I got into a fighting stance, ready to thrash the first bruiser who reached me.

Suddenly, with a loud bellowing, the enraged bull came blasting through the auditorium doors, splinters flying. He horn-hooked the pants of Bad Jace's nearest buddy, flipping him into the air and directly against the prism-festooned bowl of a chandelier, glass tinkling. The two other thugs jumped behind the coat check. The bull didn't stop, heading for the exit, nearly trampling a saloon girl who'd been hiding in the water closet and chose exactly the wrong moment to finally escape the opera house. She collapsed to her knees, then got up to flee toward the theater.

To her dismay, the bear slammed his hairy mass against the auditorium doors, ripping them off their hinges. The saloon girl screamed, side-hurdling the concession like a seasoned athlete, as the bear galloped past her and into the street, where he presumably went to chase the bull. Sarah scampered after them both, which made my stomach somersault.

"Sarah!" I called out, running after her.

To my surprise, she had the situation under control, with the help of Poppy, of course. Exuding calm and confidence, she'd tethered a cow to one of the hitching posts, a ploy that succeeded in calming the bull. He was now nuzzling the rear end of his prospective girlfriend, which made Sarah laugh. The bear, meanwhile, had been morphine-darted by Ezra the shoeshine boy and was staggering around on all fours, pacing in front of a horse trough. Soon, brother bruin emitted a yawn before lying down in the dirt, tongue hanging from his mouth in a drugged stupor.

"Well," I said, catching my breath. "Nice work, ladies. You too, Ez."

Poppy ignored me, solemnly raising her rifle to greet whoever was behind me.

I turned to see Bad Jace and his mysterious friends standing there. I still had my gun and I was ready to draw it. A crowd of Virginia City residents surrounded us, pressing close to hear our words.

Bad Jace rubbed his head, smiling, the fight taken out of him. "That was unlike any brawl I've experienced, Kid."

My clavicle ached, but I wasn't angry, the monster muted from exertion. "True for me too."

"I don't suppose you'll hand over the animals." He spat tobacco juice into the dust, but didn't reach for a rifle.

"There's a new rule from now on," I said, raising my voice so everyone, especially the miners accustomed to rough entertainment, could hear. "Animal fights are banned in this city. They're a shameful amusement and we're better off without exhibiting such blood sport."

"Hey, you're not the vigilance committee!" someone blurted.

"No one voted you sheriff!" another shouted.

"We don't even have a mayor!" from someone else.

"We only assembled a fire department last week!"

"You're right," I said. "But I'm Kid Crimson and I've saved this city from destruction twice. So I'm calling in your debt. I have one rule as Virginia City's protector and it's this: no more animal fights."

A long moment of silence ensued, the crowd contemplating my decree.

Finally, a miner hollered, "What the hell are we supposed to do for fun, Kid?"

A soiled dove—a very nice girl, I should add—stepped forward. "You'll kill us, Kid. The men need something to do besides keeping us up all night."

"Hattie, you're such a dead fish, you couldn't keep any one of us up for five seconds, let alone all night," a miner heckled her.

Hattie gasped from the utter disrespect.

Poppy trained the muzzle of her long gun on the heckler and said, "Apologize to the lady, buster."

"Oh yeah? And who's going to make me?"

Poppy aimed, pulled the trigger, and the miner's cap flew into the air. Poppy sighted, took her shot, and blew the cap all the way back to the opera house.

"I—I—I'm right sorry, Hattie. No offense meant," the man said in an abject voice, then turned and ran.

"That ends the public comments portion of our town hall," I announced.

The residents grumbled as they headed back into the saloons, including Hattie, who palm-lifted her hair coquettishly and winked at me before making her way to her cabin.

As he walked away, Bad Jace gave me a nod, our friendship intact—at least for the time being.

Poppy lowered her rifle, wiping sweat from her gorgeous brow. "Maybe we should leave for your grapefruit orchard tonight, Kid. I can't believe you banned animal fights."

"Well, I did and that's the end to it."

Wielding a notepad and pencil, Sam Clemens, intrepid reporter for the *Territorial Enterprise*, approached, doing his best to contain a guffaw. "Oh my lord and scapegrace. If I can't celebrate the cruelty of men toward animals, I'll have to produce even more political balderdash. You didn't just kill entertainment in this town, Kid. You destroyed half of my column inches."

"From what I hear," Dunn said, her own notepad and pencil in hand, "your column inches were already quite minuscule."

Eyes bright with interest, Sam said, "Young lady, I like the cut of your jibes."

"Sam, allow me to introduce you to the dime novelist Clementine Dunn from New York."

"Clementine, is it? Why, we nearly share a name," Sam said. "You know, for a while, Kid suspected me of writing all those delicious adventure stories about him."

"Delicious? You savor my work, Mr. Clemens?"

"I do," he said. "It has the flavor of imagination, concentration, and...and..." Sam trailed off, at a loss, for the first time since I'd known him, for a word.

"Narration?" I offered.

"Lactation?" Poppy didn't miss a beat.

"Compensation?" Dunn said with a slight upturn of the corner of her mouth and a raised eyebrow.

"Ah!" Sam's eyes lit up. "Yes yes yes. The Kid Crimson dreadfuls are bestsellers—or so I've heard."

She gave him a playful look. "For me, writing is a game of endurance. Every morning, I ask myself, how long can you sit here and weave words, Dunn?"

"There is nothing comparable," Sam intoned, "to the endurance of a woman. Of a woman writer, even more so."

"Well, I've had all I can endure," Poppy said with a giggle. "Let's set up these animals at my uncle John John's farm, then convene at the Blood Nugget for steaks."

"That's a magnificent plan," Sam said. "Since he's slashed my word count, I insist that Kid pays."

I laughed. "I'm happy to pay, as long as your coverage in tomorrow's edition is fair."

"Fair and balanced, without question!"

"And"—Dunn took his arm—"a little alcohol-soaked, no doubt."

4
_____

Poppy bandaged me in the back of the Sure Cure, the opium establishment she operated on C Street, thanks to my relationship with Ralston. Hers was the only den allowed on the white side of town and it made a lot of money, mostly from the hundreds of men who sought to numb their nightmares after having been wounded in war or barely escaping a mine explosion or collapse in the Comstock.

Patched up, hungry, and thirsty, we repaired to the Blood Nugget, where we joined friends in a booth that maintained some privacy, while allowing Verbena, the owner, to keep an eye on things. Jericho took a break from tending bar to cook our tasty steaks, which we devoured. There were five of us in the booth: Poppy, Sam, Dunn, myself, and Verbena. The whiskey was flowing and soon our tongues grew loose. We were enjoying ourselves…until Dunn tempered our merriment with her deadline.

"It seems the Paiute girl Sarah has influence over you, Kid," Dunn said, flipping open her pad.

Everyone went silent. Sam smirked, stared into his whiskey glass. Poppy glared at the woman. Verbena pretended to be occupied with pinning her hair into a bun. I too was a little irritated but tried not to show it.

"Sarah is a child, but wise. She's right to insist on eradicating blood sport."

Poppy couldn't help herself. "Kid rescued Sarah from a tribe on the verge of ruin, brought her here. Now she's our daughter."

"Not formally adopted, however," Dunn, relishing her technicality. "She's unofficially yours."

"If you haven't noticed, Miss Dunn," Poppy bristled, "there are no orphanages in Virginia City. Few residents are eager to take in a Paiute girl, especially one with a knack for hanging around with large wild animals—"

"Flower," I said, raising my hand to indicate she shouldn't indulge a writer's notetaking. "Miss Dunn is trying to understand me better. She has questions—"

"Exactly, such as why did Virginia City's deadliest gun ban dogfighting based on a girl's request? You must admit, Kid, that your moral code is, well, complex."

Poppy didn't drink since confirming her pregnancy, but now she reached across the table to grab Verbena's whiskey and pound it, then continued to scowl at Dunn.

"Flower, I don't think you should partake—"

She cut me off with dark daggers.

Verbena signaled to Jericho to bring another bottle. Sam offered the bartender his own unspoken signal, a request for a noose with which to hang himself. Verbena giggled, swatted the newspaper man's arm with perky admonishment.

I was about to reveal something about my upbringing to Dunn, then thought better of it. Instead, I reached for the dime novelist's drink, pounded it, and crossed my arms with mock anger, which induced much laughter from everyone and even caused Poppy to grin.

Sam made a show of pulling out his watch to look at it. "Oh my goodness, would you look at the hour. I promised I'd escort Miss Dunn to the Gold Hill, where she's staying. Verbena, do you mind, darling?"

"Of course." Verbena scooted out of the booth to allow the writers their departure.

Dunn closed her notepad and said, more for Poppy's benefit than mine, "Forgive me. I won't be so brusque next time. It was a long trip from New York to Virginia City. I'm thrilled to be here with every one of you. Good night, Kid. Thank you for dinner, Verbena."

"My pleasure."

"Good night, Miss Dunn," I said.

After the writers departed, Poppy said, "I don't trust that woman."

Verbena shrugged, pouring from the bottle Jericho had brought. "Virginia City is growing. More and more people arrive every day. Lucky for me, they seem uniformly liquor-prone."

"We're growing not just in population," I said, "but also in mythic status."

Poppy uncrossed her arms to fiddle with and fold a cloth napkin. "I don't want to be mythic. I don't want Miss Dunn to fathom my Kid Crimson. I want to grow my business, sell it to Ralston, and leave for California with my handsome husband." Upon uttering these last three words, she rested her lovely head on my shoulder.

I put my arm around her and pulled her in tight... until my bruised collarbone and cut arm pained me and I flinched. "Ouch."

"I thought you and Bad Jace were friends," Verbena said.

"We are. That's why we love to tussle."

"Who were the men with him?" Poppy asked. "Kid and I haven't seen them before."

Readying her reply, Verbena imbibed more whiskey. "Poppy, I miss my drinking partner." She made a sad face and touched my wife's hand affectionately, which I tried to ignore. The two had an interesting relationship that at times seemed tinged with Sapphic intent.

"I know, darling. Only a few months more. Unless Kid has his way with me again after I push this one out."

"That has always been the plan," I said.

The women groaned.

"So those men who were with Bad Jace? They pulled into town only last week," Verbena revealed. "Ralston hired them away from the Pinkerton National Detective Agency. They're here to form a vigilance committee, a militia created to defend Virginia City from the rising threat of bandits. Bad Jace, I imagine, is tasked with their command."

"And here I thought protecting our town was my job," I said, just for effect. I wasn't offended by additional security. I couldn't be everywhere at once. Also, Ralston had broached this exact scenario months ago. With Poppy in a family way, it made sense to relieve my burden.

"Don't worry, Kid. Ralston has a big job for you. The biggest yet, I believe," Verbena confided.

"Bigger than guarding Lincoln?" Poppy wanted to know.

"Let's not forget," I said, "the wealthy French nobleman with infinite resources who tried to blow up the silver mines with cannons a few months ago."

"Bigger than both. I don't know all the details, but the basic idea is scary." Verbena was often found in the company of men like Ralston and William Sharon, the architects of Virginia City. Her saloon operations put her in the path of a lot of information, most of it legitimate—unlike Sam Clemens who specialized in newsprint hogwash.

"Tease me," I said, "with what you know."

"Stagecoaches," she said.

"What about them?"

"They're disappearing."

I knew something about it but played along. "We've lost a few recently due to robberies, yes. I read about it in the papers, same as you."

She shook her head. "Without a trace."

"What do you mean? Stages are, what? Vanishing into thin air?"

"Wheel tracks stop suddenly on the trail, no wreckage, no burned-out shell of a carriage. Everyone on board, from the driver to the shotgun to the passengers. They're just—poof—gone."

Hank Monk had mentioned something about all this during our last trip. His line hadn't been affected, but the Cali-Nevada Company had lost, he claimed, two stages in the last forty-eight hours. No one could figure out where they went or what happened. No bullet casings or bodies or stray bullion. It was like the stages never existed, even though everyone had seen them leave town.

"Okay. Well," I said, pouring whiskey for myself. I needed a shot after hearing Verbena validate Hank's tall tale. "I already have a few theories."

"You should share them with Ralston," Verbena said, her attention drifting to a faro table where an argument was brewing. She ran a tight ship and didn't appreciate antics unless she was the one unleashing the chaos.

"We're breakfasting tomorrow," I said, following her

line of vision. A gambler had suddenly shoved the dealer nearly off his feet, demanding a refund. "Want me to handle this?"

"Poppy, would you mind terribly?"

"Not at all," my wife replied. "He remains on your payroll, Vee."

"Hang on a sec," I said, stepping out of the booth. "The two of you decide whether or not I get to do my job?"

"I'm just being polite," Verbena said, with an ironic smile.

"We love you, Kid." Poppy blew me a kiss, resting her hands on her growing and adorable belly.

"I'm bringing a steak to Grover before coming home," I said. I didn't reside in the back of Grover's undertaker office anymore, having married Poppy, but he and I remained close. Grover had been, of course, a groomsman at my wedding.

"Okay, Kid. Verbena's giving me a ride, I think."

"Absolutely," she said.

Leaving them to enjoy each other's company, I made my way to the ruffian, still making hostile gestures at the dealer. His wiry frame was difficult to perceive amid the other more robust miners and hearty prospectors filling the room. But his sun-browned face bore the creases of long days under the unforgiving desert sun. His beard scruff failed to conceal a perpetual look of weariness. Sparse strands of unkempt hair clung to his scalp. Weathered hands, calloused and stained with dirt, gripped a chipped glass of lukewarm beer. He wore a threadbare shirt and worn trousers, signs of a life spent navigating mineshafts. Despite his diminutive stature, there was resilience in his gaze, a glimmer of determination that spoke of survival amid the harsh realities of the mining town. His peripheral vision intact, he turned to square off with me. He puffed a cigar.

"Young'un," he said, "this table is occupied currently. Run along to that game of marbles behind the Dead Dice, where the milk dribblers play."

"You're making a scene," I said. "Keep it up and I'll have to escort you off the premises."

"Is that so? What's your name, kid?"

"You just said it."

The cigar fell from his lips, but he caught it, lit end up, before it landed on the floor. I made a note of his quick hands. "Kid Crimson? I've heard of you."

I tipped my hat. "You ready to move along?"

"That—why, that's a fine idea, sir." He took a few dollar bills that he'd won in the last few games and shoved them into the dealer's pocket. The dealer, smiling, seemed amenable to the size of the tip, especially after having been treated roughly.

"We do appreciate your business," I said. "If you're willing to behave, you can stay a bit longer."

"Name's Buzzard. My brother's missing is why I'm all keyed up, you see. He was unloading whiskey on the Indians and was supposed to meet me here a few days ago."

"Who's your brother?"

"Fella by the name of Gentry."

I kept my face neutral upon hearing the name of the whiskey trader Hank Monk and I had encountered on the grisly run from Placerville. Apparently, Gentry and his fresh-faced pal didn't reach Fort Churchill. Did the Annihilators catch poor Gentry and Joaquin?

"Tell you what. I have contacts in the area. Let me find out what they know. I'll relay it to you when I hear something."

"Appreciate it, Kid. Sorry for being a bother."

"You work for one of the bigger mining outfits, Buzzard?"

He shook his head. "Just a prospector hoping to hit a streak before I get too old to push a sluice box. All I need is one little vein."

I patted his shoulder, which freed up some dust, and gave the dealer a look, indicating he should let Buzzard win a hand or two. He nodded his assent.

Then I went to the bar and ordered six uncooked T-bones from Jericho.

"Sure you don't want those cooked?" Jericho said, making change for my greenbacks.

I shook my head. "They're not for me."

———

BAG OF STEAKS under my arm, I took the darkest route, just beyond the streetlights, where the moon offered minimal illumination and cruel numbskulls would be eager to throttle me. It didn't take long for them to approach, blocking me from reaching Grover's Graveside Services.

Four men, each of them with a leashed bull terrier, straining and growling low. They wore cattleman hats and long dingy coats—collared ankle-length dusters—that made it difficult to determine what weapons, if any, they carried.

One of them stepped forward. "You went too far, Kid, bringing that Paiute girl into our town. There's real money in blood sport and your decree turned us into paupers."

"I'm sorry to hear that," I said. "But you'll have to find another way to support yourselves in Virginia City."

"Told you he ain't gonna listen," another one said. "He's a wild animal that Ralston was too slow to neuter. You know, like a pit dog that you predict is gonna bite you, but you convince yourself you can control him in time. But you cain't. You cain't control a wolf."

"I hear you," said the one who'd spoken first. "That's why I have dogs—to sick on them wolves that don't follow the law of the land."

"You mush-brained knuckle-draggers don't represent the law," I said. "And as far as the land is concerned, you all wheeled up in here less than a month ago with your animals. I know you're operating a puppy mill and when I'm through with you here, I plan to set all those poor creatures free to live with Sarah."

"His talking," said the one who'd compared me to a wolf, "is starting to hurt my feelings."

"Kid, *you're* the blood sport now." The four of them at once unleashed their dogs, and four robust, big-boned animals came rocketing toward me.

But I was ready. I gave a sharp commanding whistle to dampen the mutts' instincts, then tossed the steaks into the space between us. They snapped and snarled at one another, tearing into the meat, their teeth cracking against the bones, clueless about the fate I was about to deal to their owners.

The men began to slap leather—but again, I was ready.

I hunkered down and blasted my Colt, sending two of them to Boot Hill. The third and fourth dogfighters got off a few rounds that whizzed close and as I side-shuffled, I did them wrong by gut-shooting one and neck-clipping the other.

"Damn it," the gutshot dogfighter squawked. "He's too fast!"

The throat-gouged fellow could only gurgle.

They both died moments later.

Ezra, the shoeshine boy and my adopted son, emerged from the shadows, visibly disturbed by what he'd seen. His eyes were big, brewing with tears. "Kid, that was...that was incredible. I thought...I was sure—"

"Leash them up," I said, motioning toward the dogs, sitting on their bellies, gnawing down on the cow vertebrae, comfortable with the present arrangement and ignorant of their own fate. "These boys are due for John John's farm."

Ezra tethered the animals in the span of a few seconds, having learned a thing from his animal-wrangling girlfriend Sarah. "That place is getting crowded."

"Not as crowded," I said, "as the graveyard."

5

I MADE EZRA PROMISE NOT TO TELL POPPY about the carnage. I didn't want to keep secrets from my wife, but certain conflicts I needed to handle on my own. The men I killed wouldn't have rested until I was dead and I couldn't leave Poppy a widow, my kids fatherless. I knew Ezra recognized this on some level and his insistence on following me wherever I went wasn't a trait I cared to break. He'd saved my life during a hot-air balloon battle last year, which solidified my trust in him, earned slowly since I met him. In fact, I had more faith in him than in any man walking the streets of Virginia City. Ezra was a fantastic kid and a good soldier. Even though he observed my most violent side, and he was all of eleven years old, his code was solid. He was like me, a romantic who couldn't be swayed to do ill by the devils around him.

I hadn't told anyone the real reason I gave the impulsive command to end animal fights. Even Poppy didn't know. I grew up hurting other kids, a child pugilist in the kid-fighting circuit across the South, a revolting form of entertainment that drew the scum of the Bible Belt, dark-hearted men titillated by the sight of boys making other boys bleed…and worse. When we were done hurting one another, the same men descended on us, pretending to want to bandage us, mend us.

What they did to us then was far viler than what we'd endured in deep fighting pits of red clay which had been dug by slaves so that spectators could look down on us, hurl abuse, throw trash, spit and urinate on us, on our open wounds. When I saw a dogfight, it brought back memories of myself at age nine, scared out of my wits, my soul shredded by my father's hatred of me, his only son by a woman who had passed for white, but ended up, to his horror, producing a son with slightly duskier skin than his.

She was Seminole, so was I too, good for nothing more than the fighting pits. He educated me only to torture my brain, to make me acutely aware of the cruelty he inflicted on me. My father enjoyed looking into my eyes and detecting the anger and the shame and the sadness, aware that I knew just how completely broken I was—mind, body, soul.

He was a thorough bastard.

I slept fitfully that evening in a big white bed, my beautiful Poppy beside me, my bandaged arm throbbing. I didn't miss my nights in a satin-lined coffin in the back of Grover's Graveside Services. But I *did* feel the loss of the extended evening talks with my surrogate father. I still briefly chatted with him most mornings, after escorting Ezra and Sarah to the brand-new schoolhouse Lydia Sweet had secured financing for earlier in the year. It was an adorable one-room structure of desert pine, painted white with the Union flag flying high atop a pole in the small backyard.

I could've used such a place when I was growing up and I'd have preferred it over the one-to-one ministrations of my tutor from Paris, a frog-eating, cigarette-addicted pedant who was never satisfied with my Latin tenses. If anything, his snobby instruction enhanced my disdain for the drawing room and had me dreaming of riding horses and shooting bottles off a fence. However, I was grateful for his insistence on me reading Alexandre Dumas's *The Count of Monte Cristo* and *The Three Musketeers*.

It was Poppy who ultimately civilized me. Together we resided, with Sarah and Ezra, in a three-bedroom house rented from Ralston on A Street, where the well-heeled enjoyed all the comforts of civilized existence. Grass yards. White picket fences. Buggies and horses. Our neighbors were assayers, ore processors, and insurance directors, and though Poppy was Chinese and I had some tribal ancestry, they treated us with respect and greeted us with smiles and verbal niceties. They knew better than to do otherwise, I guess. I wouldn't have tolerated any other attitude.

Poppy's cousin Sing lived with us too, the young man charged—in addition to cooking meals—with caretaking our two wild urchins. Indeed, Sing's main job was to keep them from running the two short blocks down the hill to C Street and stirring up trouble in the evening. They needed to be fresh for school. They complained about homework, but they adored their teacher, Miss Sweet, and I loved how, despite all the commotion and filth that Virginia City generated, Sarah and Ezra enjoyed in many ways an ordinary childhood at a time when the world was war-rationed, weary, rotten.

Still, the citrus orchard was my goal. I wouldn't rest until I saw my children zig-zagging through rows of trees bursting with green leaves and yellow grapefruit tinged with pink. Another big job from Ralston and I'd have enough to realize my dream of taking my family to California for a better life, where guns would never find us. Where love was ours as long as we wanted it.

Hopefully, Ralston's money would take us far, far away from this wasteland.

He was waiting for me, as always, at a table in the Griddle of Doom, my favorite breakfast spot on C Street. But he wasn't alone. A familiar and repulsive figure was sitting beside him—Eli Sackmary, the useless gemologist who found shovels to be anathema to his line of work. Hair damp from a morning bath, he resembled a drowned weasel.

"Good to see you again," I lied, shaking his limp hand. "And in less extreme circumstances."

"I was just telling Ralston," Sackmary said, "about the Cisco station incident and how you navigated us to safety."

Ralston had already ordered, knowing how I loved the chocolate chip pancakes. He sipped from a steaming mug of black coffee. "I wonder if this outfit Eli mentioned— the Annihilators—is connected to our disappearing stagecoaches."

"I'd like to learn more about the disappearances," I said. "What can you tell me?"

"First, let's have a bite of breakfast. Losing money tends to stoke my appetite."

After wolfing his eggs and biscuits, Ralston began describing the mystery, which was pretty much how Verbena outlined it. Days ago, two Wells Fargo-backed investment bonds heading for Virginia City left San Francisco, en route to Placerville via stagecoaches. Both simply vanished, leaving no tracks along the trail, no personnel or passengers located thus far, no sign of the horses. It was as eerie as it was final. Complicating matters was the fact that Ralston had lost his best book-keeper, Skinker. Returning from San Francisco, he disappeared with the money and everything else.

"Have you considered Skinker as a suspect? He might've slaughtered everyone and buried them some-where in the vast Nevada desert."

"Yes, I did consider him," Ralston said, tucking into his own pancakes, chewing slowly, yet never ceasing to speak. "But Skinker has the mindset of a bookkeeper and lacks a conspiratorial bone."

Sackmary was making a mess of the perch and eggs he'd ordered, the thin and elaborate bones of the fish flummoxing his clumsy fork and knife efforts. "This is supposed to be a whitefish…at least I think so."

"Yes, the perch in Washoe used to offer a brighter and softer meat," I said. "But as mining runoff increases, the flesh gets darker and grittier."

"It tastes the way gunpowder smells," he said, disappointed. He tried the scrambled eggs, which stayed on his fork and seemed to please him more.

Ralston leaned over to inspect Sackmary's plate, then shrugged before dispatching the rest of his pancakes. "In any case, the financial losses are significant, but not crippling. Stagecoaches evaporating into thin air, however, can't continue."

As edacious Ralston was with his stack, I was equally reverent of my own. "What about the missing passengers? Anyone important?"

"Second-rate entertainers, from what we can gather. A soprano. A magician. And a boxer."

"That's a full calendar of events. No wonder poor Myles had to put on an animal fight in the opera house."

Ralston grunted in reluctant affirmation, polishing the syrup from his fork with a napkin before placing the utensil next to his crumb-less plate. He was a thorough eater, like myself, if a little hasty, which is why I didn't take what he said next too personally. "Heard about that fiasco. I'd appreciate a heads-up, Kid—before you go changing the rules in Virginia City."

I took my last bite, savoring the chocolate chips and ignoring his request. "Tell me about the magician. What's his specialty?"

"Escape artist. At least that's what the poster said."

"The newspapers claim the magician is among Lincoln's favorites," Sackmary added, giving up on his osseous breakfast.

"The president is a magic enthusiast?" I hadn't heard this biographical detail before.

Ralston nodded, giving the waiter a moment to refill his coffee before speaking again. "Since childhood, when he used to entertain school chums with tricks he learned from books."

I pondered this. "What's the magician's name?"

"Thurston Larue, the Shadow Man."

"The Shadow Man?"

Sackmary sipped his coffee, making a face that suggested he didn't care for that either. "Larue walks the line between reality and the imagination."

"Sounds like Mary Shelley," I said.

Ralston seemed intrigued. "The name is familiar."

I reached for my coffee. "British author who wrote a book about a monster reanimated from pieces of the dead. It's called *Frankenstein*."

Ralston deprecatingly waved away my mention of a fiction. "What's your interest in the magician, Kid?"

"Magicians often have a desire to make people—and things—disappear."

"Like the stagecoach, you think?"

I shrugged. "I'll ask the Shadow Man when I find him."

Sackmary scoffed. "Good luck. Did you not hear Larue disappeared without a trace?"

"There's always a clue somewhere. Thanks for breakfast, Ralston. I'll need a few items from Roscoe's House of Hammers." I rose from my chair.

"Hang on, Kid. Look, Pinkertons crawled all over that route. They found nothing."

"Well, they didn't crawl it with Snake." I donned my hat and took my coat from the portmanteau behind me.

Ralston absorbed my statement. "Your Paiute accomplice. The one who brought reinforcements to Virginia City in time to defeat the Confederate Frenchman."

"Yes. Snake is an expert tracker. He'll require a stipend too."

"I'll authorize it. You've yet to let me down, Kid. I'll put the money in your account, and you can pay him out of that sum."

"By the way, why is he here?" I said, pointing.

The mincing gemologist furrowed his brow at my question, napkin-wiping the corners of his mouth. "Kid," Sackmary said, "you're a significant expense on the profit-and-loss statement, and I was curious about how you went about incurring these costs. I learned a great deal from this conversation."

I still wanted Ralston's answer. "So Sackmary is replacing Skinker?" I could tell by the look on his face that he appreciated neither Sackmary's speaking for him nor what he divulged.

"Filling in. Temporarily."

"In that case, I hope he doesn't intend to introduce cost-saving measures."

"There's no price," Sackmary intoned, the implications of our speaking about him in the third person completely lost on him, "on preserving the Union. After all, Lincoln needs silver to finance his campaign. Ralston claims you can be counted on."

"I don't give an alligator's nuggets about the president's nightmare crusade," I said, hearing my angry Southern accent creep into my voice. "The industrial North slaughters poor agrarian whites with one hand tied behind its back. What we do here in Nevada won't shape the outcome."

Ralston seemed to bristle. "So why *do* this work, Kid, if you don't believe?"

"I have significant expenses," I said, "on my own statement; a citrus orchard in California and a baby in Poppy's belly."

An epicurean in his own right, Ralston understood this, his head vaguely nodding. "Well then, I'll make sure you get what you need to secure your farm once the war is over. I promise you."

I didn't let on that I had no intention of working for him that long. As soon as I had enough money, I'd be gone. My heart was full and there was only room for Poppy, Ezra, Sarah, my son on the way, and Grover—the people I cherished. There was no room for the Union. I'd die for my family if I had to and it wouldn't bother me in the slightest. But my cherished dream was to take my loved ones to California, to drag them from the dark cave of Virginia City and bathe them in the light of day.

Would they recognize the scary beauty of reality and be strong enough to avoid retreating to the manacled darkness of this filthy mining town? I hoped so.

And I hoped to live long enough to bask in the sunlight with them.

6

AFTER BREAKFAST, I HEADED OVER TO HOUSE OF Hammers. Smiling and singing to himself, Roscoe was in a jovial mood when I set foot inside his notorious hardware store. It was really more of a stocked armory for the irascible residents of Virginia City, where law enforcement was a dream and firearm ownership a dirty yet necessary reality. Indeed, without easy-to-acquire guns, bad men would've had their way and good men would've been at their mercy.

Claim jumping had soared in the days before Roscoe's arrival, a time when bandits roamed the Comstock, searching for a miner with a sack of gold, then gang-shooting him to acquire possession of the dead man's parcel and mineral rights. Sure, Bad Jace was in the process of organizing a vigilance committee, but members of that group were akin to an after-the-fact and far-too-late clean-up crew and not at all like steadfast peacekeepers.

There was no jail in Virginia City, the closest hanging judge gaveling men's lives away in Reno. Guns were the equalizer, allowing an outnumbered prospector or a petite soiled dove a fighting chance to protect earnings and limbs by bullet-piercing a violent rapscallion. Roscoe felt guilty at times that his store served as the spot where a jilted lover or a wrathful poker player might instantly purchase, say, a two-shot Derringer and cause havoc.

On the whole, though, House of Hammers prevented our town from spiraling into chaos. Weapons made us honest in our daily interactions and uneasy about being rude toward others when we didn't know who was armed and primed to snap. We had to credit House of Hammers with balancing the odds for well-intentioned men.

"You seem happy today, Roscoe," I teased him. "Have you found a lady to tangle with?"

"I did, Kid," he said, raising his arms to place his finger-laced hands behind his head. "She's beautiful and kind and cooks up a storm. And she loves me! We're getting hitched and I'm attending temple every Sunday until our wedding this summer."

"Wow, she sounds perfect. What's her name?"

"Emma Christensen."

I couldn't believe it. Emma was the girl who'd shown me a measure of affection in Goblin Valley before Rocker Portwell had provided a tour of his cannon foundry. I'd heard her supposed beau, Elder Wilford, had gone back to Utah, but not that Emma hadn't. "Roscoe, you're really marrying a Mormon girl! I thought you were being lighthearted about your aims last we spoke." I slapped his arm with buoyant warmth. "Congratulations, you old brush wolf!"

He gave me a wink. "I mean, she's not as a stout as I prefer them, but—"

"Roscoe Judd, this isn't a salty miner's trench where you can speak illicitly about your fiancée!" Emma emerged from the back room, smiling in a dress of softened pineapple leaf with large, loose-gathered, bishop sleeves, her blonde hair smooth and lustrous and pinned up. She was radiant and lovely, obviously enjoying her stint as her soon-to-be-husband's assistant.

"You're working here already?" I said, laughing. "Emma, I'm so happy for you!"

"Kid, I'm happy for *you*. Look how healthy you are!"

She was referring to the knife Prince Polignac, the Confederate commander, had thrown into my ribs, nearly collapsing a lung. Lucky for me, I healed faster than a desert lizard. "Thanks to you feeding me pasties in my time of dying, I actually managed to recover."

"Oh, I didn't bake them, of course. Our mutual friend Winifred is terrific in the kitchen. I'm better with a Dutch oven on the trail.

"I could use your cooking these next few days. I'm off to California tonight."

"Good," Roscoe said. "I was worried your ban on animal fights landed you on someone's kill list. There's a lot of money in blood sport."

"Enough nonsense," Emma said. "Kid is on a job for Ralston. What can we sell you, honey?"

On a job for Ralston? It was clear I'd have to reconsider who was the proprietor and who was the assistant.

"Well, uh, I was going to ask Roscoe..." I gave him a look, but he didn't offer a lifeline. Instead, he crossed his arms and raised his eyebrows, feigning amusement that I hesitated to request a weapon from Emma. "Fine. I'm looking for a pepperbox pistol, something I can conceal inside a stagecoach, but with more wallop than a Derringer."

"Pepperbox, hmm," she said, turning to survey the guns mounted on the wall behind her. "Here's a six-barrel Allen & Thurber. It's thirty-two caliber and punches hard." She scooted a ladder to a spot underneath the weapon she'd described, grabbed the hem of dress with one hand, climbed a few rungs, and pinched the revolver off the nail from which it hung.

"Emma," I said, "I had no idea you were versed in firearms."

"Rocker always had me and my brothers practicing drills in Goblin Valley." Rocker was the dreaded Mormon enforcer—bodyguard for and confidant of the late Joseph Smith—who I'd teamed up with months earlier to repulse Prince Polignac's assault on Virginia City. Emma and Rocker had escaped Illinois and joined the same temple in Utah, where they'd been building cannons for Lincoln, until I showed up. "But I'll admit, I'm better at cleaning guns than hitting targets." She used both hands to gently lay the pepperbox on the counter between us.

I picked it up, admiring its design. "They call this a muff pistol in England."

Emma nodded. "On account of carriage-riding women hiding it in a poofy mink-furred hand warmer. They use it to thwart bandits lurking amid the gaslit cobblestones."

"You're starting to make me jealous of Roscoe, Emma," I said, winking at the shop owner as I returned the pistol to the counter. "Unlike *my* wife, you know a lot about guns."

"Come on, Poppy is a crack shot," she said. "With a Winchester, she hits anything she sees."

"You mentioned a stagecoach," Roscoe said, concern in his voice. "I suppose you're helping Ralston to prevent more of his deposits from disappearing."

"Along with the stages, the horses, and all the people on them, I bet," Emma added.

"I'm helping Ralston, yes," I confirmed. Sometimes I had to share a tidbit in order to acquire new information. "I heard the entertainers were riding the stage and just, well, melted away without a trace."

Roscoe glanced around the store to make sure no one else was eavesdropping. "Emma and I met a magician named Thurston Larue at the Gold Hill Hotel before he departed. He was an interesting fellow, young and high-strung."

"He drank furiously and shared strange stories, Kid," Emma said.

"Like what?"

The couple shared a look. Then Roscoe began to wrap the pepperbox for me, leaving his wife-to-be to explain.

"He bragged of surrendering to the Confederate army —not once, but three times."

A head-scratcher, for sure. "What on earth for?"

"He apparently enjoys sneaking out of prison," Roscoe said, writing up a bill of sale for my tab. "Fancies himself an escape artist."

"He got away every time?"

"Yes," Emma said.

"Did he explain how he does it?"

"By disappearing into thin air," she said, handing me the pistol wrapped in beautiful pink crepe yarn and wax paper.

I tucked the elaborately packaged gun under my armpit and headed toward the door. "Well, like you said, he seems like an interesting fellow."

"Don't vanish with him, Kid."

"Oh, I'm too loud to fade away."

"So true," she said, smirking. "You nearly deafened

all of us while saving Virginia City from Confederate cannon fire."

"That was nothing. I can get much noisier."

Roscoe harrumphed. "Yeah, well, nothing booms like a pepperbox inside a stagecoach. Take care with the pistol, Kid."

"I will. Thanks, and congratulations on the wedding. I hope you're inviting Poppy and me."

"You made it possible for Roscoe and me to meet," Emma said. "You and your wife are at the top of our list!"

"I like being on *that* kind of list."

———

I HAD to say goodbye to someone before leaving town, a man I held in high regard, a father figure I suspected was disappointed in his errant son. When I arrived, he was doing what I'd expected—puffing a cigarette and reading his King James on a stool in the back of his coffin shop. As always, two or three mutts were gravitating toward a pool of formaldehyde in the alley. Grover kept an eye out and when a dog got too close in an attempt to lap at the poisonous puddle, the undertaker picked up a rock and threw it at the animal.

He saw me approaching and his body language was conflicted. I discerned that he wished to step forward and embrace me, but a part of him also yearned to smack me on the side of my head. He satisfied both impulses by reaching out with his cigarette hand, while looping the finger of his other hand through his belt loop. I let him wrap his smoky arm around my neck and, with barely contained exasperation, exhale in my ear. "Did you have to kill all four of them, Kid?"

"They were playing for keeps, Grover."

He shoved me away suddenly, half-playfully, and though I didn't smell alcohol, he looked like he'd been drinking. "I buried them in the same grave, since they carried no identification. No one claimed them or offered to confirm who they were. But everyone knows those men had started breeding fight dogs. Poppy's uncle has them now on his farm with all the other creatures you're collecting, including an elephant."

"Thanks, Grover. Let me cover the cost." I reached for my billfold.

"Put it away, Kid. You're upsetting me."

I did what he instructed. "Hate to ask, Grover, but did any more bodies show up? Maybe from the trail?"

"You out there killing bandits now?"

"I'm looking for specific folks—a singer, a boxer, and a talkative magician."

His anger softened as he realized I was seeking passengers on the missing coaches. "I would've alerted you if I had. Or I would've sent Ezra and Sarah to tell you after church."

Grover took them to Sunday school. To his credit, he'd asked for our approval. He knew about my brutal upbringing in Georgia, that my relationship with God was fraught, and how I didn't want to perpetuate the abuse my father had inflicted on me. At the same time, he cut me less slack these days. Now, as a father and husband, if I killed someone, it had to be for a good reason. He could no longer downplay my violent instincts, because my actions had consequences for my family—and for Grover, serving as a kind of grandfather to Ezra and Sarah.

I could see myself from his perspective and I didn't blame him. He was my replacement father and he loved me, Poppy, and our children. We loved him just as fiercely. But I didn't have enough money to realize my dream. I needed more and Ralston had offered the job that would allow me to finally pull up stakes. I intended to bring Grover with us to California, but was he willing to leave Virginia City behind? Sometimes I wondered if his occupation as undertaker was an obsession rather than a profession. Perhaps he despised the world as I did and sought to bury as many people as possible before his own end. Was an unspoken and shared hatred for mankind the basis of our bond? Was I the mechanism for death and he the resolver? Maybe he'd convinced himself that reading his Bible would lessen his guilt at having ended up a funeral director in a mining town.

I'd let enough time pass after he'd mentioned church with the kids, so I asked him for the favor I needed. "Still have the spirit coffin?"

He looked at me, picking tobacco from his lips. "Yes. The schoolteacher, Miss Sweet, returned it to me last week after Ezra brought it to school and scared his classmates."

I laughed. "Do you mind if I borrow it for a spell?"

He arched an eyebrow. "As long as you don't give it back to Ezra."

"I won't."

Grover led me through a door that led into the embalming room, where the air was thick with formaldehyde, and alcohol mingled with the faint scent of decay. There was a large cast-iron stove in the corner of the room, its door ajar, glowing embers within. Grover used the stove to boil water, the heat worsening the room's oppressive environment. Nearby, a worn wooden cabinet housed his more delicate instruments, including glass bottles of scarce chemicals. Inside this cabinet, hidden away from prying eyes, was the spirit coffin, a small wooden toy of a casket, the size of a beer glass. A friend had given it to him after graduating from a mortuary school in Ohio. The trick was simple. You showed the audience the empty coffin, holding it open like a book. Then you dropped a piece of chalk inside and closed the lid. The audience heard the sound of the chalk moving inside the box, and when you opened it, a spooky message was always written inside the coffin on the interior panel.

Grover handed me the magic trick and I slipped it into my coat pocket.

"I'm mighty curious, Kid. But I'll let you keep your secret."

"See you in a week. I'm off to locate a missing wagon. And I want to say thanks again."

"For what?"

"For taking Ezra and Sarah to church. I'm grateful you're here to guide them, especially on the religious front."

"God hasn't given up on you, Kid. He doesn't give up on any of us. Until it's too late."

I didn't have the heart to tell Grover I didn't care either way. That I'd revisit our relationship only if God let me reach California with my family intact.

I had a hunch though, I'd have to kill plenty more bastards to get there.

7

I STOPPED IN THE SURE CURE TO KISS POPPY goodbye. She didn't like spending too much time in the opium den now, believing the vapors might harm our baby. Poppy's uncle John John had assigned his nephew-in-law, a conscientious young man named Lip Shee, to manage the place. But Poppy felt if she didn't check in at least once in the evening, the whole place might fall into an unprofitable, irrevocable abyss. She was waiting for me outside on the boardwalk, dressed in a bright-orange silk-brocade mandarin gown that flattered her curvaceous figure and enhanced her breathtaking femininity. Her adorable kidskin leather slippers, with yellow floral needlework, made me want to snatch her like a war trophy and whisk her to Hunter Creek Falls for a weekend of prolonged and lascivious frolicking. It brought immediately to mind how I observed her that morning pad across our bedroom naked and barefoot, one delicate hand on her rounded belly, as she scooped silk drawers from her dresser. It charged my desire for her to a degree that I hadn't been able to shake since.

"This missing stagecoach business is a distraction," I said. "I want to steal you away for further impregnation, so we can have two babies instead of one."

"Not how biology works, Kid."

Poppy put her arms around me, standing on her tiptoes to give me a delicious kiss. She tasted like saffron and cinnamon and the impending reality of not having her in bed beside me for the next several nights made my bones ache. Only Poppy could cure my afflicted mind rattling with nightmares and bloodlust. Only she could quiet the monster that stirred inside waiting to be unleashed. I hated the monster, but I acknowledged it was because of this deadly demon that I remained alive today. How could I banish something that had saved me countless times, plus my family and Virginia City, from destruction by evil men? After I transplanted us—Poppy, Sarah, Ezra, Grover—to the grapefruit orchards, would I be able to keep the beast tamped down? I didn't pray, but maybe I'd pick up the habit in California. If He'd listen. If He cared enough about me, given all the blood I'd spilled.

"I don't know much about biology," I said, kissing her soft mouth. "But I know one thing, my little flower."

"What's that, Kid?" She wrapped her arms around me, pressing her face to my chest.

"I can't make it without you."

"You don't have to. We're here for you, Kid. All of us."

"Why, though?" I grabbed her arms and stepped back, studying her face. "I've turned the town against us."

Poppy smiled. "The residents here are greedy and ignorant, yes, but they still know the difference between right and wrong. Most understand that blood sport is cruel. It's why they haven't burned down our house."

I blew out a relieved breath. "Chaparral and Bad Jace have an eye out for you and the kids while I'm away."

"Don't worry about us, Kid. Finish your mission. Find out what happened to the stagecoach. Come back safe." She removed my hat, running her gorgeous fingers through my sweaty hair. "Try not to get killed. Or even wounded."

"Snake is joining me. He's death on two legs, so we can't fail. And Poppy?"

"Yes?"

"Am I too much? Is living with a killer...too extreme?"

"You're not too much. And I'm not married to a killer. You're the only man in the West who's honest with himself, truthful about how the world gouges us."

I didn't quite figure how to respond. So I asked a question. "Will I cut it as a farmer?"

Poppy didn't answer. With a tender expression, she kissed me one last time and started walking back to the Sure Cure.

———

WHEN I REACHED THE LIVERY, the six-up hitch was harnessed to a freshly shellacked Concord and ready for a stagecoach ride. Hank Monk was brushing the coats of the elegant horses, hackneys and Welsh ponies. He loved animals, another reason he and I got along so well—as compared to my other travel companion Bad Jace, who took sick pleasure in sniping coyotes from the buckboard and chuckling darkly when he dropped one. Whatever, Bad Jace was now Lydia Sweet's problem, along with the children who attended her one-room schoolhouse. Hank and I weren't morally superior to the lumbering brute. We were just better at not lashing out at defenseless creatures when we needed to let off steam.

"Have you met my friend Snake?"

Hank shrugged, continuing to give attention to his animals. "Not that I'm aware, but I've run from my share of Paiute. I'm sure he's chased me and struck my coach with arrows."

I laughed. "Snake doesn't chase Concords. He prefers pin cushioning settlers and miners."

Hank swallowed nervously. "He's one of them Pyramid Lake marauders?"

I didn't want to lie to my driver. "Yes. He's killed many whites. He was upset, naturally, about them chopping down all his trees. The Paiute rely on nuts and berries for food."

"How—how many did he kill?"

"A few dozen," I offered a conservative number.

Hank was eager to change the subject. "I know the route the missing coach took. It's a doozy."

"Why do you say that?"

"The trail runs through Devil's Gate, a half-mile stretch of high-walled, rock-strewn cliffs."

"Perfect spot for an ambush."

"Well, that's not all," Hank went on. "A steep slope through there gives you no choice but to slow your team. And Devil's Gate is so narrow you can't turn the coach around."

I whistled at the challenge of this scenario. "Why the heck did they run investment bonds through there?"

"Quicker route. Trying to cut corners, I guess."

"They cut their own necks. You knew the driver?"

"Young fellow from New England named Charlie Parkhurst, but people call him Darkey. He's not one to be trifled with, I tell ya. Can't see anyone ambushing him. He's fast and shoots back."

He wasn't fast enough and didn't shoot nearly enough bullets, I wanted to say. "Just gone, huh?"

"Disappeared. Along with that magician you asked me about."

"How long has it been since you took Devil's Gate?"

"I stopped taking that route months ago. Too many robbers."

"They never took a single shipment of yours, is what I hear."

Hank nodded. "True, but they gave me plenty of gray hairs. I don't need any more."

"Gray hair is a blessing," I said. "Ask any bald man."

"Ha. It's not the aging that bothers me, Kid. It's the anxiety."

"What makes you anxious, Hank?"

"Growing older and losing speed."

"You're as fast as ever."

"Maybe. But stagecoach driving is like gunfighting."

"How so?"

"Slow down enough and you're dead."

"You're in no danger of slacking off, Hank."

"One day they'll catch me."

"Hopefully that day is a long way away."

"What about you, Kid? You're pushing twenty-five now."

"I only get faster, more accurate."

"How's that, I wonder."

"It's due," I said, "to my family. I can't relax the pace until I know they're safe in Sonoma County, enjoying the ranch and the grapefruit orchard that I bought them."

At first, Hank didn't respond. Finally, he commented, "Will you be there to join them?"

I looked right at him. "If I'm not, what's the point of all this?"

———

WE LEFT Virginia City under the cover of darkness, heading in the direction of Devil's Gate, the rugged and narrow gorge where we'd been told Charley Parkhurst had disappeared. Less than four miles from Virginia City, Devil's Gate offered an irresistible chance for bandits to raid a stagecoach or for an ambitious illusionist to attempt a disappearing act on a massive scale.

According to Hank, whenever a driver had trouble on the trail, it usually occurred in the narrows. Refusing to risk it added considerable time to a transport, but Hank rarely took this route for fear of banditry—hence, neither had I. Once beyond the rugged, metamorphic rock, however, a stage passed easily enough through Silver City, Empire, Carson City, Genoa, and Van Sickles Station, before climbing up the Kingsway Grade to Dagget Pass, then descending through Strawberry, Placerville, and Shingle Springs, and finally to Sacramento. I didn't expect us to have to make it that far to find Parkhurst or the magician, but I wanted to reach Fort Churchill, on the California border along the Carson River, to determine the fate of Gentry and Joaquin, the whiskey traders Hank and I had whupped at the Cisco station.

"Thanks for your help," I said to Hank, bandanna covering my face due to all the dust.

"Well, you are paying me, Kid. Handsomely."

"Sure, but this is dangerous work. At least compared to working for the Overland company."

"Every job in Nevada is risky."

I couldn't argue with that. Instead, I looked out at the horizon, searching for warning signs, puffs of dust, movement in the cliffs. All I saw was night's long dark curtain over everything, cooling the desert in preparation for another sun-drenched Nevada morning. All we heard was the wind blowing eerily through the canyons and, barely intelligible over nature's din, our own chattering voices, tuned to the key of anticipation.

We sat side by side on the driver's bench, talking things over and reminding ourselves of other journeys, other mishaps and adventures. During lapses, I searched my mind for pictures of Poppy, Ezra, and Sarah eating dinner at the table in our house, laughing at something ridiculous a particular shoeshine customer said to Ezra. I recalled every slat of the white picket fence that perimetered our home, the little green patch of grass in the front yard, the hammock hanging from the two pinyon pines, the only remaining trees on the entire block, everything else having been chopped down for firewood. I was a fool for leaving my beautiful family to locate Ralston's missing stage, even if it only took a few days. I trusted Chaparral and Bad Jace to protect Poppy from harm, yes, but her heart needed shielding too. I was a whelp, waving my gun around to bend the world to my will, to force it to accept my dream, small as it was. I believed myself clever enough to pistol-whip the West into giving me money to escape the pain into which I'd been born. Part of me was tempted to share my feelings with Hank on this and other matters, but he wasn't an ideal set of ears. He was a gifted talker, not a listener, and when he launched a story like the one he was spinning now—a tale about how he'd encouraged drunk men on C Street to throw snowballs at a burning saloon—it was difficult to interject or make him stop.

He needed to stop, because three riders on the trail ahead were galloping straight at us.

Chatty as he was, he was always alert and had seen them before I did. With the reins held loosely in one hand, he reached for his Winchester. "And that's how the Virginia City Volunteer Fire Department first formed. Grab your shotgun, Kid."

"Think they'll charge us off the trail?"

Hank spat chaw. "They can try. Pinks, you think?"

"They have the look, even from this distance."

They drew closer, and in the moonlight, I saw the men wore dark clothing—gray jackets, single-breasted vests, pressed trousers, wide-brimmed boleros. Their horses were narrow-shouldered dun-colored Kiger Mustangs that looked menacing, manes flowing wildly in the wind. The men wore pistols on their belts—clunky but powerful Colt Walkers. Their rifles were scabbarded, so I didn't draw down on them. But with our body language and glares, Hank and I made it obvious we were ready to give them the business if they sought to rob us. We had nothing, of course, but they didn't know that. They pulled in their reins, halting their horses on the trail, blocking us, the one in the middle raising his hand elegantly, indicating he wanted to talk.

Hank looked at me, and I nodded.

"Whoa!" he said, yanking the coach's brake lever and bringing us to an abrupt stop.

Dust billowed around us, each party waiting a beat for it to drift away. Then the man who'd waved finally said, "We're with the Pinkerton Detective Agency. You routing to Sacramento?"

"Show us your fancy badges," I said, unwilling to take them at their word. I'd had run-ins with Pinks over the years and the experiences were never positive. They believed themselves master spies, even when they blew their cover and got innocents killed. Given carte blanche by Lincoln to root out secessionists and Uncle Toms, they exerted more effort in tormenting illiterates than foiling actual conspiracies. Worse, the agency tended to attract broken men who enjoyed bullying the weak instead of taking the fight to the real threat—wealthy financiers who supported the Confederacy, men like my wicked father. Indeed, money made Pinks look the other way and find softer targets and it sickened me. Pinks weren't professionals; they were thugs with powers granted to them by a president who won less than forty percent of the vote.

The three of them shared a sour look, until the spokesman said, "You didn't ask nicely, runt."

I cocked the hammer on my flintlock, a loud and distinctive sound. "That nice enough?"

The man grunted, reaching carefully inside his jacket to yank a piece of metal off his vest. He tossed it under-hand at Hank, who caught it.

He studied it, but I already saw that it was legitimate, the top of the brass badge bearing the all-seeing eye, along with the Pinkerton motto: "We Never Sleep."

Hank lobbed it back at the agent and said, "What can we do for you?"

"We're looking for a stagecoach that disappeared in Devil's Gate. Know where it is or who might've stolen it?"

I kept my face neutral, knowing I was under the scru-tiny of three so-called detectives. But I frowned to myself. Now I had the additional challenge of hunting a vanished carriage that the Pinkertons were seeking at the same time. What had Ralston lured me into?

"We don't know anything about a lost stagecoach," I

said. "We're on our way to Placerville with mining documents. If you'll kindly move aside, we can still get there expeditiously."

"No passengers?"

"None," Hank said.

"Mind if we take a peek inside? We're looking for a specific gentleman who might be traveling under an alias."

I shifted my weight in the shotgunner's perch. "We told you this is a commuter-free ride."

As if on cue, a sneeze issued from inside the carriage.

The agents seemed greatly amused by this turn of events. Not angry, just entertained.

"Excuse me," I said, climbing down, so I could reveal our stowaway, something I hadn't planned for and that threatened to upend our mission.

I grabbed the door handle and swung it open. Inside, handkerchief pressed to her face, was Clementine Dunn, the pretty dime novelist.

She sneezed again.

"Bless you," I said.

"Damn me," she said.

"I won't argue with you about that, Miss Dunn."

"Mistress, actually."

"Lord," Hank said, rubbing his face while still clutching his Winchester. "Surrounded by Pinks and the world's deadliest gun, while trafficking a married woman without her husband across state lines. My job gets harder every day."

"NAME'S BANGS," SAID THE PINKERTON, leaning forward onto his pommel. "My colleagues are Crumb and Lennox."

Crumb, the stouter of the three, tipped his hat. Lennox sat motionless and stone-faced in his saddle, unimpressed by what was in front of him. It wasn't an act and I took an instant dislike to him.

Hank was about to speak when Bangs cut him off. "*You're* Hank Monk, famous stagecoach whip. And *you*," he said, looking at me, "must be Kid Crimson. Heard about your exploits down in Arizona."

"Didn't know the Pinks had a branch office," I said, helping Clementine out of the coach.

"We don't. I'm from Chicago, but spent time in Tucson fighting Indians and bandits."

The friendlier one, Crumb, spoke. "Pleasure to meet you, Kid. You saved the silver mines here, not once but twice. Is it true you jumped from an air balloon to land on another?"

"I'm his official biographer," Clementine said,

brushing road dust from the sleeve of her dress that I'd inadvertently smeared on her. "And it's all true."

She wore a powder-blue embroidered-mesh tulle gown and a pair of boy's cowboy boots that ignited a lust in me strong enough to mute my irritation with her for having hitched a ride, and with the Pinks for delaying my investigation.

"She's *not* my biographer."

Clementine clucked her tongue, still addressing the agents. "I can tell you everything you've read about him in the press is a denuding of his unrivaled bravery. I confirmed everything myself, including the balloon feat of derring-do, by interviewing residents of Virginia City who witnessed him in action firsthand."

This was enough to make Lennox smirk. "Denuding. That mean you seen him in his britches, warts and all?"

"Lennox," Bangs warned. "Don't do this. I can't help you if you—"

"Kid has no warts as far as I know," Clementine huffed, redoing her hair with a pin. "He's happily married to a beautiful young businesswoman in Virginia City."

I was already squatting to pick up a rock when the agent continued his nonsense.

"I heard," Lennox said, "that his wife's an opium trollop with a den right on the main—"

I hurled the stone at him, clipping his forehead and knocking him off his horse, his hat flying.

I removed my jacket and handed it to Clementine, then rolled up the sleeves of my shirt, cracked my knuckles, and walked over to Lennox, dazed, lying in the dirt and groaning. He propped himself on one hand, while using the other to check his face for blood. I stooped to grab his shirt collar and wound up for a backhand when I heard a hammer click as Bangs pointed his Colt Walker at me. "You made your point, Kid. Lennox has a mouth and you shut it for him."

Hank raised his Winchester at Bangs. "Enough grab-ass. Let us finish our route, so we can get paid. Besides, your badge ain't valid in the Territory of Nevada."

Bangs slowly relaxed the hammer and holstered his pistol. "We'll join you as far as Empire."

"Why accompany us?" I said, having released Lennox so he could cough and sputter in the dust.

"We're looking for the same thing."

"What makes you think that?" Clementine said, returning my jacket to me.

"Kid Crimson is too lethal a shotgunner to be guarding documents. He's a special-missions type and I'd bet a bar of gold that he's after something—or someone—committed to undoing Virginia City's financial contributions to Lincoln."

"Oh, who might that someone be?" Clementine asked sweetly.

"A member of the Knights of the Golden Circle, naturally."

"In Nevada?" I said. "Unlikely."

"The war creates improbable scenarios, Kid. Consider the fact that you, a Georgia boy, find yourself in Virginia City doing jobs as if you're, well, a Pinkerton agent."

"I'm nothing like a Pinkerton." I clenched my jaw.

Bangs recognized that Lennox's attitude had ruffled me. "Forget it. Look, we're searching for the same stage. We've scoured the narrows, but maybe we missed something. Let us double back with you."

I scanned the jagged lava rocks erupting from the horizon behind the mounted agents. "Tell you what. We'll follow you into the narrows as the sun rises. I have a suspicion about how the stage vanished. If I'm right, a few extra guns will be useful."

Bangs nodded. "Sounds good. We have a few hours until dawn. I suggest we rest a spell."

"I'll get a fire going over by those junipers," Hank said, snapping his reins to move the stage off the trail. I knew he'd soon start feeding the horses, then loosen their harnesses so they could sniff and paw the grassy spot he'd chosen.

"I'll give you a hand," Crumb said, trotting over to the trees to tether his Kiger.

By this time, Lennox was back on his feet, dizzy and chastened as he struggled to don his hat. He turned his attention to Clementine. "Sorry for my rudeness, ma'am. I haven't slept in two days."

"No offense taken, sir," she said, grabbing his arm to steady him. "Would you like a drink?"

"I sure would appreciate one, ma'am," he said, wiping his face with his sleeve and avoiding my glare.

Clementine went to retrieve what I assumed was a flask from the stage and I joined her.

"What are you doing here?" I hissed in her ear. "This job isn't safe for a writer. And why are you rewarding that fool with whiskey?"

"How do you expect me to write a compelling adventure story about you, Kid, if I don't witness you in the thick of it?" She offered me a drink.

I took a sip and had to admit it was decent. "You sold plenty of stories without ever having met me. And I didn't ask you to write anything. Tell me why you really traveled all this way."

She sighed. "New York publishing has taken a sinister turn. Lincoln continues to arrest newspaper editors. The government is starting to censor dime novels. In fact, the stories about you are considered a threat to the war effort. Let's face it, the West is where true freedom still holds. I'm out here to get a better look at it—and you."

"Let me get this straight. The fairy tales you write about me somehow undermine support for the war in the North?"

She nodded. "Honestly, I embellish very little. I take what's printed in the *Territorial Enterprise* and goose it only slightly, presenting it as fiction."

"I thought I was supporting the Union by protecting its silver in Nevada."

"You most certainly are. However, it's your adventurous spirit, Kid—your refusal to sacrifice yourself for any cause—that puts you at odds with the powers that be."

Flabbergasted, I took another sip of whiskey, then another. The kick from the alcohol felt divine, but it wasn't enough to resolve my confusion. "No good deed goes unpunished."

"Sorry I snuck aboard," she said in what seemed like a little girl's voice. She stepped forward, delicate fingers straightening my cravat. "I wanted to ask permission, but I knew you'd refuse."

"Apology accepted after this business is settled. But I thought you and Sam were getting along. Now suddenly you have a husband somewhere…in New York?"

"Sam is a jovial soul, but he's working a story. And there's a fetching darkness to you, Kid, that women can't resist." She brought her lovely face close to mine. "I—I don't think I'm exempt."

I removed her glasses, folded them, and placed them in my coat pocket. Her eyes, glassy now, lost their ability to focus. She was blind as a bat. "Who's your old man, Clementine?"

"Kid? I can't see too well without—"

"Tell me his name." I placed my hand on her soft throat until I could sense the shape of her windpipe. Her breath was warm and smelled of peppermint oil and good whiskey.

"Emmett. Emmett Kinney. He serves as an officer in General Burnside's Ninth Army Corps." She raised her hands to grab mine, which were squeezing her throat. To my surprise, she pressed down hard on my fingers, increasing the pressure, her eyes moist and submissive.

"That's a decorated unit. The Ninth has fought in multiple theaters. What's a dainty scrivener like you doing with a lethal soldier?"

"We met in Philadelphia. He attended military college, while I was a student in the design school. We were nineteen when we married. Things between us collapsed before he left to fight the Rebs." She was out of breath now, my grip inhibiting her breathing, but she didn't push me away. Instead, she pulled me closer, her lips grazing my chin. "Oh, Crimson," she whispered.

If I'd had time, I would've resisted the moment, but I was powerless against her rushing force. My mouth sought her lips and she gave willingly. Was it a second or an eternity? However long it lasted, she tasted like a candied apple glistening in greenest Eden. Still, something was wrong.

"So your husband's alive then," I said, breaking it off and pulling back my hand.

"As far as I know." She rubbed her throat almost sensually.

I returned her glasses. "Give that yappy Pink some whiskey. I'm not buying a word you say, just so you know."

She donned her eyewear and nodded, staring at the

ground for a moment to gather herself before walking over to where the agents had tethered their horses. They were talking with Hank, who was already tending a fire, about Indian-fighting tactics, which revealed to me they weren't particularly adept at hand-to-hand with the Paiute.

Soon Snake would arrive, presenting a challenge—namely, how to keep my Indian friend from stabbing the Pinks with a flint knife while they slept.

———

CLEMENTINE CATNAPPED IN THE STAGE, while the rest of us dozed on the ground. None of us slept well, but as I gazed up at the stars, I thought of where the missing stage was likely hidden. A coyote yipped. A few yards from my blanket, a jackrabbit stood up on its hind legs to sniff the air. Soon, dawn started to glow on the horizon and as we prepared to navigate the narrows, we resembled scarecrows patching ourselves with straw in all our weakest areas. Hank coughed up his morning phlegm and spat it into the dying embers. The Pinkertons used a canteen to splash their faces and, with bicarbonate powder, brushed their teeth, leaving their mustaches chalky.

"I'll take some," I said, extending my open palm.

Bangs nodded and sprinkled a spoonful into my hand. I'd never minded my dental hygiene on the trail, which needed to change. I hadn't lost a tooth yet, though, even after Snake had elbowed me in the face years ago during a fight near Pyramid Lake. When Clementine emerged from the stage and caught me using my fingers, she touched my shoulder and handed me a toothbrush.

"I can't use yours."

"Brought an extra," she said. "I'm not a primitive like the rest of you."

I rinsed with my canteen before offering it to her so she could brush with the mint oil she'd brought along.

"Thanks," she said. "Ready to find the missing stage?"

"I am," I said. "Hopefully these Pinks won't get in my way."

"They seem...deferential."

"Not of me. Just my résumé."

"Which I explicate in the dime novels based on your adventures."

"These men don't read."

Clementine shrugged. "Their wives and girlfriends do and they tell their men."

"I rather enjoy the notion of women in the Northeast cuckolding their husbands with a Kid Crimson story and sharing details with them later."

"Now you're getting it." She laughed.

I laughed, too. Clementine exuded frippery and charm. My buddy Sam Clemens, the *Territorial Enterprise* reporter, couldn't help but be in love with her.

In minutes, we were all galloping hard toward Devil's Gate. I sat in the gunner's perch, to the right and slightly above Hank and Clementine, turning around every so often to make sure no one was boxing us in. There was the briefest fuss when Lennox, riding point, reined his horse. He drew his gun at something in the road, blasted it once, and rode on. The other two agents trotted past, not even bothering to look at what their colleague had shot. As Hank and I passed the site, we spotted a rattlesnake, its head blown off.

Hank whistled and said, "Lennox ain't too shabby with a Colt Walker."

I said nothing, making a note that the agent I'd toppled could actually hit a target.

With the Pinkertons in the lead, we pushed into the canyon, wind singing a broken song through the rocks, notorious for serving as a hideout for highwaymen and robbers, making a trip through the Gate's narrows unsafe for travelers. The *Territorial Enterprise* often published reports of people being relieved of their watches, wallets, and other possessions as a "toll" extracted by unsavory types lying in wait within these barbed stones. The jagged terrain looked, if you squinted your eyes a certain way, like the dreadful maw of Lucifer himself, his teeth ready to masticate pilgrims on their way to Silver City, on the canyon's other side.

While we paused at the forbidding entrance, Hank said, "Don't suppose you Pinks found stagecoach tracks when you came through here yesterday."

Bangs shook his head, not bothering to turn around in his saddle. "The powerful zephyrs wipe the sand clean through these narrows."

Crumb added, "You know, Silver City miners claimed they heard an explosion as they were threading this place, but no debris was found, no smoking wagon ruins. But the miners couldn't be sure, after all—"

As if completing his sentence, a distant yet loud detonation filled our ears, a gunpowder boom designed to carve deeper into Ophir Peak. Hungry for silver ore and desperate to make good on their investments, men came to Nevada to cause mayhem deep in the earth in exchange for extracting riches. Losing a stagecoach full of money seemed, at least to me, like a small inconvenience in a larger, more threatening landscape of bursting rocks and mercury poisoning.

"Lots of explosions," Clementine said, "in this part of the world."

About a quarter-mile inside the slot, I found what I was looking for, a significant expansion in the rock face, off in a pocket where horses and wagons wouldn't need to tread. I told Hank to halt the stage and climbed down. The agents stopped and turned their horses toward me, curious to know what I was up to. With the stock of my flintlock, I tapped the area, pacing back and forth across the length of the dusty patch where no rocks stood, finding nothing.

"What are you looking for, Kid? Landmine?"

"Hank," Clementine said, "why would Crimson blow us up?"

"I don't mean *that*. Maybe they used a mine to disintegrate the stage and covered it up?"

Finally, I struck something solid. "Grab the shovels from the stage boot, Hank. You, too, Pinks," I said to our armed escort. "I think I hit a jackpot."

I was returning to Hank's stage to help him get the equipment when out of the corner of my eye, I saw it.

The pike. Swinging out from behind a boulder.

It hooked Crumb, who'd just dismounted, tearing into the back of his neck. He emitted a chilling scream as the killer used the stone as a fulcrum to see-saw him up in the air. Crumb kicked his legs wildly, trying to generate momentum and wriggle free. But the sharpened pole had pierced him expertly and he went up in the air like a circus act.

A bruiser with a hand-cranked gun strapped around his neck like an accordion stepped out from behind the same rock and pointed the barrel at poor Crumb, smashing the agent with at least a dozen .58-caliber rounds that blew his right arm off, then severed his leg before the rest of the bullets pulverized his skull and chest. The pike never dropped, holding the corpse aloft like a gruesome, bloody piñata.

Lennox's horse reared in fright, causing him to lose his balance and fall off his saddle into the dust. He landed on his back, wind knocked out of him.

Bangs, meanwhile, raised his Colt Walker, but before he could squeeze off a shot, a leather whip snapped the weapon from his hand, then cobra-cracked the bridge of his nose, blood splattering.

I fired both rounds of my flintlock at the man with the coffee-mill gun, but the ammo hopper was so large it doubled as an armored shield. The killer peeked over it to offer a revolting smile.

I reached for my Colt Army Model 1860 single-action revolver, intending to wipe that grin off his face, when the whip came my way, snatching my gun, then my legs out from under me. And then I felt the pressure of the pike's metal hook on my trousers, dragging me toward the Annihilators.

"Kid!" Clementine screamed, bunching her skirt so she could run toward me, save me from my doom.

"Clementine! Don't—"

Something hard bashed my head and I lost consciousness.

9

"HE HAS A SKULL LIKE ANTHRACITE," I HEARD Snake say. "But an undersized member. That's why I call him Tiny."

"I doubt he's lacking in virility," Lennox retorted. "Women can't seem to get enough of this here jasper. I think it's because he's packing. And, obviously, he's a pretty boy."

Snake grunted with disapproval. "At least he fights well. Though in this instance, not at all."

"It was an ambush, I tell ya," Lennox insisted. The three of them came out of nowhere. Like they knew we were coming."

Snake grunted. "White men?"

"Looked like from what little they showed of themselves. Had the whiff of Texas on 'em."

"Kid sent me a telegraph warning me about a gang called the Annihilators."

"Heard of 'em. The agency never had a fix. Supposedly they did a job for—"

Bangs interrupted. "Lennox, don't share information with random Indians."

"I'm not random," Snake said. "My people have been here and fought for this land for too many years to count. You sound like Chicago though, which makes *you* happenstance."

Bangs, sighed. "Sorry, Mr. Snake. I was making a point about Lennox offering particulars collected by Pinkertons to someone who isn't, well, a Pinkerton."

"Apologies, Bangs," Lennox said. Then he asked Snake, "Where'd you learn your English?"

"Missionaries."

"They teach you to shoot like that too?"

"Of course not," Snake scoffed. "Gunnery I learned from my grandmother."

"Well, you seem to have had an interesting upbringing, Mr. Snake."

I started to get feeling back in my arms and legs. The sensation of a cool, wet cloth on my forehead was comforting, but I had a blinding headache. I tried to sit up, but lightning struck behind my eyes. I was lying on the desert floor, for how long, I had no idea. Through painful slits, I could barely see that I was in the shade behind a boulder. Whether I'd been pike-dragged here or carried by Snake and the others, only they knew

Managing to raise a hand, I started to explore my scalp, feeling for cracks, holes, fissures. Other than sticky wetness, I seemed to be intact. Once again.

"He's alive," Lennox said. "I can't calculate how a man survives a wallop like that."

Squatting next to me, Snake removed the cloth from my brow and wrung it out in the dirt. "Kid isn't a normal man. I learned this when I tried to kill him at Pyramid Lake. We barely had fuzz on our nuggets when we stabbed and shot each other. We fought to a standstill. Someone else clipped him with a bullet and he fell into a ravine. Ever since, he's been my responsibility."

Lennox was quiet a moment before saying, "You go on a lot about people's nether regions."

"I have no idea what you're talking about."

I laughed, which made my head throb even worse. "Lord, what a conversation to come around to," I croaked, my throat dry as sand.

"You missed the earlier back-and-forth," Bangs said, his nose gauze taped. "When the Annihilators had the advantage. Lucky for us, Snake here arrived. If not for him, we'd have wound up like poor Crumb, piked and blown to bits."

The sudden silence gave my head a brief chance to clear. "Where are Clementine and Hank?"

"Annihilators took them in the stage, heading toward Silver City."

"Dang. What are those lunatics after?"

Snake stood up and pointed. I finally sat up, even though my poor noggin was moiling my neck, and strained to see.

"This patch of soft limestone on the canyon wall?" Snake offered. "Marked with a sharp piece of quartz. You'll recognize the sign of the Knights of the Golden Circle."

"There it is again." I raised my arm for Snake to pull me to my feet and he obliged. Dizzy and spiraling into an awful funk, I took a sip from the canteen Lennox offered me.

"You must've seen that symbol," Bangs said, "at the Cisco station. The family that ran the place was killed there. You and Hank found them."

"You know about that?"

"We checked it out, thought it unrelated, but now it's clear the Annihilators are after you. And they're sending you a message."

I drank more water and explained. "Hank and I didn't discover the murders. We discovered two whiskey traders, Gentry and Joaquin. Said they'd clashed with the Annihilators, losing their crew. They scrambled to Cisco for shelter and found the family already dead."

"Where are they now?"

"Fort Churchill, I think."

Bangs shook his head. "Doesn't matter. We need to recover Hank and the girl."

"Well, she's the Kid's biographer, so I'm sure he wants her back," Lennox said. "I guess she writes his hijinks down and publishes them in those thin dime Western books that are all the rage with the ladies back east."

"You go on a lot about Kid Crimson's female admirers," Snake said.

"I have no idea what you're talking about."

Watching the tension develop between Lennox and Snake got my blood flowing enough to get ready to jump between them if I had to. But Bangs saw it too and managed to defuse the situation by saying, "Kid, you were about to show us something before you got clobbered."

"Yes, I was," I said, still glaring at Snake and Lennox, warning them off and buying me a little time to get my thoughts straight. My first impulse was to head down to Silver City and rescue Hank and Clementine. The thought of the Annihilators having their way with the dime novelist stoked the monster inside me. But I was in no shape to fight and my marching orders from Ralston were to locate the missing stages.

Looking for my shotgun, I spotted it beside a pinyon tree and picked it up. All my ammunition was on the coach, so once again, I used the stock to sound the sandy layers of the dilated pocket in the canyon. In the bright morning sunlight, I now noticed black powder burns etched into the surrounding walls, evidence that someone fairly recently had blasted. I'd unloaded a shovel from the wagon before the Annihilators commandeered it and with it I scooped away the sand, about an inch deep, off the top of what ended up being the headframe at the top of a mine shaft, along with what I assumed was a hoist and a sheave wheel.

The men grew anxious as I began to shovel more sand off the iron lid, revealing an abandoned shaft that probably hadn't been recorded by any Assay Office. As more of the lid came into view, Bangs and Lennox joined in the unearthing, getting on their hands and knees to push pebbles and debris with their gloved hands, fascinated by what was taking shape.

Snake held back, sensitive that whites had violated his ancestral land. But I could see he was curious.

"It's heavy, boys," I said. "Help me open it."

At this point, Snake contributed by lighting a fire with some kindling and a small magnifier I'd bought him last year for his birthday. Lennox, Bangs, and I heaved the lip of the cover, iron hinges screeching as the cool air of the shaft hit our faces. That surprised me. Mines tended to be warmer than the air outside, so the shaft likely connected to a cave system beneath Devil's Gate. I didn't recall anyone ever discussing this in my presence. I'd have wagered there were multiple access points to reach the underground caverns in the slot canyon and that Ralston, at least, knew about what lay beneath this eerie bridge between Virginia City and Silver City.

Bangs gathered a branch and a scrap of poor Crumb's uniform, then dipped it into Snake's fire before handing me an improvised torch. "Think the Annihilators dropped the stage into this pit?"

"No, they simply wheeled it down the angled slope," I said, illuminating the chasm below and the steep ramp leading into a well of darkness.

"What we're lookin' at," Lennox said, "is crazier than popcorn on a hot skillet."

"Please," a woman whimpered in a wretched voice. "Help us."

———

ALL FOUR OF us had been kneeling to inspect the shaft and squinting into the abyss when the woman startled us. We yelped and leaped to our feet, then looked at one another, brave warriors scared by a soprano.

"The earth is calling you, Kid," Snake said.

"Not the earth. A nightingale. I have a hunch who might be down there."

Snake gestured for me to go ahead and confirm my suspicion.

I bent down again to say, "What's your name?"

"Nora Pearl!" the voice cried desperately. "Left here to die by demons!"

"Were the demons three men from—"

"Get us out of here!" she cried. We're out of water and food."

"Who's we, Nora?"

"A man named Con Orem. A boxer."

"Bareknuckle fighter," Lennox commented, squatting next to me. "Irish boy. Born in Ohio."

"We're throwing down a rope, Nora. You come up

first. Tie it around your waist and make sure the rope is in front of you."

"I understand."

With that, Bangs knotted together a few lariats from our horses and dropped his rescue line into the black maw. Still wobbly, I let Lennox and Snake slowly pull Nora "Nightingale" Pearl up the ramp of gravel and crushed stone and into the light. She emerged, a lost yet fluttering angel, crawling out of the depths of a desert underworld. She was the loveliest mess—hair wild, face covered in dirt, purse clenched under her armpit. Squinting, she shielded her blue eyes from the harsh daylight before collapsing on her hands and knees.

"Water," she sobbed. "Hurry!"

Bangs was ready with a canteen, giving her small sips, careful not to let her overdo it. Meanwhile, Snake and Lennox dragged the bareknuckle brawler out of the hole in the ground. He was shirtless and shoeless, his muscles sweating, and seemed much worse off than Nora. None of us asked what had happened to his footgear, but Lennox could barely contain himself.

"I saw you fight a Scot in Cripple Creek, Colorado, last year," he said to the pugilist. "I won money on your bout and used it to entertain a soiled dove."

Con Orem lay flat on his back, forearm over his eyes, breathless from his climb.

"Lennox," Bangs scolded. "You're talking too much to someone in dire need of your canteen."

"Oh. Of course. Here. Have some water, Mr. Orem."

Lennox assisted the boxer by propping up his head so he could drink.

With the exception of Orem struggling to breathe, we all sat together in a rough circle for several minutes.

Nora Pearl showed improvement, so I said, "You're lucky to be alive."

On the verge of tears, her voice trembled. "I can't believe you—anyone—found us."

"What happened?"

"Terrible *terrible* men dropped on us from the canyon walls. They took an evil pleasure in torturing and killing the driver. Then they rolled the stagecoach into the bottom of the cave—"

"Was anyone else with you?"

"Oh. Yes. A magician. They took him with them."

"The magician went willingly?"

"They seemed to know him."

"Go on."

"Then they pushed the boxer and me down into the darkness. I sprained my ankle. Con Orem fell harder, twisting his back. We survived on some food and water in the stage."

"Must've had plenty."

"There's another carriage down there. A man named Skinker, badly injured, had been shoved into the mine, and died."

Ralston's bookkeeper.

"Hopefully, Con Orem survives," I said.

Nora Pearl took another sip of water. "He has a fight tonight in Silver City with a big purse."

This seemed to excite Lennox. "A fight? Tonight? You know, I believe he's never fought in Nevada before. Isn't that right, sir?"

The fighter made no reply, eyes blinking with exhaustion, lips chapped and cracking.

"He's not doing well," Snake observed. "Needs a doctor."

"Lennox," I said, "we need you to take Con Orem to Virginia City to see Scullard."

"He your town sawbones?"

"When he's not drinking. Well, even when he is."

"They all do. The war breaks their minds, I think."

"Kid," Bangs said, "you should go into Silver City with Snake and me."

"I was planning to, Bangs."

"But not as Kid Crimson. You go in disguise as Con Orem."

"Disguise? How could I do that? And why?"

"Chances are the Annihilators are in Silver City or Empire or any of the neighboring towns."

"So?"

"So when they hear the boxer they believe dead is suddenly alive and stepping into the ring, they'll be curious. They'll show up to the fight, where Snake and I can take them down."

I considered his idea for a moment. "I'd prefer to focus on rescuing Hank and Clementine."

"Sure, and this is how we flush them out."

"You're a good boxer, Tiny," Snake said. "The Pinkerton's plan might work."

Lennox didn't hide his disappointment. "Shucks, I'm going to miss the fight?"

"Yes," I said, "but you'll be with your new friends, Con Orem and Nora 'Nightingale' Pearl."

"Okay," he said, "here's ten dollars. Place a bet for me."

"Thanks, Lennox," I said. "I'm flattered."

"Not on you. On the other fighter, Tom Molyneaux. He's a black fellow who punched his way out of slavery in Virginia and into the sporting section of all the newspapers."

"Fine. But I keep half the winnings if I lose."

10

We fashioned a stretcher that could be dragged behind a horse to bring Con Orem back to Virginia City. Nora Pearl rode the horse, with Lennox walking alongside, making sure that the horse walked slowly, Orem didn't jostle too much, and Nora stayed upright.

Then Snake, Bangs, and I buried what was left of Crumb.

We washed up in a ravine on the Silver City side of Devil's Gate, and the three of us navigated our horses down the bustling main thoroughfare in Silver City. I donned Con Orem's shabby top hat and jacket and handed Bangs my iron, hoping to pass for the touring boxer with daunting fists. A disguise turned out to be mostly unnecessary. The population of 8,000 carried themselves despondently, their posture akin to whipped dogs, their spines hunched as if enduring heavy burdens. They were an embittered, abused version of the hopeful creatures of Virginia City, at least by comparison. Silver

City was a town of broken souls who didn't care who showed up, as long as they paid up.

I hadn't spent much time on this side of Devil's Gate. After all, a silver rush the likes of which hadn't been seen since King Solomon's time was underway on the eastern slope of Mount Davidson, a lively and risky area that required my brutal services day and night. Silver City, on the other hand, boasted large foundries that Comstock miners relied on to process ore. The stamp mills, situated along the Carson River and powered by steam engines, hammered day and night, generating a horrific din that made Virginia City sound like a sparrow colony.

There was, too, an abundance of boarding facilities for animals, the beasts used to haul ore from the rich veins to this nightmarish town, a glorified freight center with enough saloons on the block—I stopped counting at twenty—to inebriate the combined armies of Grant and Lee. Upon setting foot into Silver City, I no longer felt guilty about bringing up Ezra and Sarah on B Street, one measly block, physically and metaphorically, from the iniquitous C Street.

The trip here confirmed the grass was greener on our side of Devil's Gate. I'd forgotten how blessed I was to reside in a boomtown brimming with ambitious men like Ralston, instead of being banished to a waystation overrun with humans and animals, the stench of a wasteland ravaged by mercury and cyanide hanging in the air like an eternal curse. Indeed, I was reminded that I'd been lucky to have landed in Virginia City instead of this sulfuric pit.

Such a reminder was nearly worth suffering a beatdown at the hands of a champion boxer.

I was still shaky from getting cold-cocked by the Annihilators. Tom Molyneaux would pummel me if

Lennox was accurate. However, one element in my favor was prodigious experience. As talented as the black pugilist might be, he hadn't fought for his life as a boy in the swamp pits of the Deep South like I had. More than likely, Molyneaux had battled other untrained slaves in informal bouts on plantations, but not as a child, more as a teen or even older. Heck, I might've even seen him scuffle a time or two, given how much my father loved to watch blacks beat one another to a bloody pulp. Months ago, in a gambit to destroy the silver mines with cannons, Prince Camile Polignac, a formally trained boxer, had challenged me and lost. His prize-fighting skills couldn't match my ability to tap the white-hot rage that boiled inside me. I eventually dropped him on his tailbone...just before Sarah dispatched him with her pet lion Uru, who ripped open Polignac's throat.

The workers' bunkhouses were unspeakably drab and decayed. Bone-weary men now poured out of them like addled crustaceans. Some made their way into the bath-houses to scald the grime from their bodies before the big boxing match in the largest sawdust-floored saloon in town, the Camel Hump, named after a failed experiment by the US government to use dromedaries from North Africa to haul cannons across the desert south-west. Two of these exotic beasts paced back and forth now at the entrance of the Hump, each ridden by a scantily clad dove—powdered and painted and dressed in exotic finery and more than a bit soiled—moving seductively to music no one else heard. An intimidating ape-faced saloon bouncer in bowler hat and suspenders, muttonchops freshly oiled, and shirt sleeves rolled up to display his veiny forearms, carried a Winchester off to the side of this spectacle. He stared angrily at the hooting men, signaling that if they tried to touch the women, they'd be cut in half.

"This place," Bangs said, "resembles a whorehouse in hell."

"My woman Estrella runs a brothel and isn't afraid of much," Snake said. "But I doubt she could bring order here. It's too wild."

"No Indians allowed in town," a local ruffian sneered from the street, pointing a finger at Snake, trying to get a mob going. "Get lost before we scalp you."

What a greeting. I didn't give the fool a chance. I hopped off my horse and gut-walloped him.

The man groaned, puked a stream of liquor into the dust, and fell over.

"Yep," said an old timer, observing me. "That's Con Orem, just like I told you fellows."

Everyone around him cheered, and before Bangs and Snake could pull their guns, a cluster of suddenly bois-terous men hoisted me into the air. In that moment, the energy shifted, desperate joy suddenly rippling across the town, starting right at the spot where I'd punched the discourteous buffoon. I didn't panic and there was no sense in resisting. After all, I was being welcomed by the working men of Silver City who viewed me as a white hope, primed to finally demolish a black champion. Ironic, since I was only half-white, pale enough to pass for Mediterranean or Spanish ancestry.

Whisked off the street, I rode these strangers' shoul-ders through the batwings of the Hump, ducking my head just in time to avoid cracking my already-damaged skull on the jamb of the doorframe, until they planted me just outside a makeshift ring, bordered by steel-wire mining ropes in the center of the bar beneath an ornate, quartz-festooned chandelier the size of a stagecoach wheel. The men stripped away my jacket and shirt, shredding them not out of anger but with drunken admiration and fervor. The ambience was raucous and brothel-like, red oil lamps casting sinister light and shadow upon a sea of eager faces, each turned toward me —and the other shirtless figure standing in the opposite corner.

The man's face was shrouded in darkness as he threw punches in the scarlet murk, preparing for a clash that would pit us against each other for the amusement of braying lunatics, spilling their drinks and laying down bets, screaming at the bookmakers in green coats and tweed caps who held fistfuls of money and scratched down numbers on scraps of newspaper.

The bearded and bald-headed referee stepped forward wearing a bowtie, white ruffled shirt with gold cufflinks, beer-splashed dress pants, and debris-caked miner's boots. The din excruciating, he beckoned me to enter the ring and, taking a brief opportunity to scan for Bangs and Snake and coming up empty, I complied, stepping carefully through wire sharp enough to lacerate skin and designed to discourage pugilists from running away or clenching an opponent.

I sized up Tom Molyneaux, still shadowboxing, and I didn't like what I saw—not at all. Gathered outside his corner, the men yelled bloodthirsty and racist epithets at him, hoping to stoke him into a frenzy so he'd lay me out in seconds, giving them an easy payday.

Molyneaux was an inch or so taller than me with a long reach I'd have to evade in order to land punches. I wasn't afraid to get in close and weather blows, but the danger lay in getting pushed back and caught up in the wire. He was broad about the neck and shoulders, suggesting his gloves would hit like sledgehammers. He lacked a cornerman and when he brought his meaty hands to his face, I noticed scars on his knuckles. Stomach like a washboard, Molyneaux seemed unbothered by the roar, the cacophony of voices tuned to the key of carnage. Perhaps he ignored the noise because his ears were cauliflowered, damaged by a life spent brawling. In other words, Molyneaux was an ideal fighting specimen and in perfect condition. He was at his peak; I wasn't.

But I didn't need to be in top shape to destroy a fighter. The monster chewing its way out of me was enough.

As I reached the center of the ring, the ref grabbed my arm to pull me in and holler, "Gotta cornerman?"

I shook my head, but then spied a familiar visage in the crowd, an impish sportswriter I'd nearly put out of business back in Virginia City—my good friend Samuel Clemens. He was smirking, notepad flipped open and pondering what to jot down next, eyes wide with surprise, incredulous at the sight of me stepping into a ring to impersonate Con Orem, a famous boxer, albeit one who hadn't made it this far west before, meaning no one knew what he looked like. Only Snake and Bangs and I knew that the real Con Orem was in Virginia City by now, recovering from being tossed down a mineshaft in Devil's Gate by the Annihilators and left to die.

"Wait!" I said. "That man there!"

The ref turned to look at the immaculately suited Clemens, then shouted into my ear, "Um, beg pardon, but he doesn't seem like he knows boxing!"

"No, but he's very funny though. I need him to keep me laughing."

The ref shrugged and waved Clemens into the ring. Holding onto his derby hat as he stepped through the wire, my newspaper buddy smiled out of sheer confusion and yelled at me, "I imagine you'll share a delightful story with me!"

"Sam, I need your help surviving this ordeal first!"

"Me? How can I assist, Crim—I mean, Con Orem? Other than by not revealing your identity."

"Don't let Molyneaux beat me into oblivion."

"Why not call on Snake?" he said, tucking his notepad into his coat pocket. "I spotted your Paiute accomplice in the crowd, along with a Pinkerton detective."

"They're here to intercept Clementine's captors. She tagged along with us and there was a skirmish, I'm afraid."

Sam's eyes widened; his fists clenched. "My dear Miss Dunn is a distressed damsel?"

I started to say something, but then a kid Ezra's age and size pushed past me, and I almost grabbed him by the collar to tell him he should be in Virginia City, protecting Poppy and Sarah. The urchin drop-slid to his knees and chalk-scraped two lines, three feet apart, on the wooden floor.

"Toe the line!" he shrieked above the chaos, then clanged a copper pan with a horseshoe, alerting everyone that the fight was about to commence.

"Will you help me?" I yelled at Clemens.

He smiled. "The trouble isn't in dying for a friend. It's in finding a friend worth dying for!"

"Thanks, Sam!" I said, feeling a bit ashamed for having smooched his love interest.

We watched Molyneaux saunter into the center of the ring to stand on his side of the chalk, fists raised and ready to inflict pain. He was utterly confident and coiled to strike.

"Good luck, uh, Con!" Clemens offered me the glass he was holding. "Thirsty?"

"You drink water?" I took a sip.

"I don't. That's straight vodka."

It burned, and I was tempted to spit it out. But I muscled it down and slapped his shoulder. "Never change, Clemens. Never change."

The alcohol infused me with bravado. I made my way to the center of the ring. My opponent stood on the other side of the chalk, eager to wreck me.

Molyneaux and I stared each other down, the monster inside me realizing it had an excuse now to revel in destruction and dismantle the bruiser piece by piece. I felt a gleeful wrath turn knots in my stomach, forewarning the monster's approach, his complete possession of me. The monster yearned to wield me as his instrument of sick pleasure. It was always the same feeling, but now, desire thickened the saliva in my throat, an aspect of sexual ecstasy making me queasy. I didn't like it, but the darkest part of me yearned to experience the pleasure of breaking another person.

"No gouging! No biting!" the referee shouted. "Fists only!"

"You gonna die, white boy," Molyneaux growled over the noise, his white teeth grinding.

"And you're about to suffer for your bread. Like a slave."

He winced at the word, then studied me, brow furrowed, and said, "You ain't Irish, not even Black Irish! You sound educated. Also, I hear Georgia in your voice. You ain't Con Orem. Who am I really fighting tonight?"

"Ten rounds!" the ref called out to the incensed audience. "No stopping unless someone slips in blood! Con

Orem the blacksmith versus Tom Molyneaux the black freedman!"

"I'm the devil," I said to Molyneaux, "from your ugliest dream."

He smiled. "You funny, white boy. Gonna die, but at least you funny."

"Round one!" the ref announced and the urchin horseshoe-bonged the copper pan.

Molyneaux crouched and snapped his massive fist, grazing the top of my head. I counterpunched, landing a wrist-deep left to the ribs that made Molyneaux grunt, then missed a right to the chin, which he side-stepped, scraping his back along the wire ropes. He hissed in pain, narrowing his murderous eyes at me.

The canvas was spattered now. I could smell the blood.

With no room for footwork and uncertain lighting plaguing my sight, I was reminded of the swamp pits I was dropped into as a child, where I fought other children as men laughed and smoked cigars and guzzled whiskey. I could feel myself blinking rapidly now, as vivid memories flooded my mind, images of boys' faces twisted in agony as I punched them again and again. One boy, I recalled, begged me to stop, and I didn't, knowing if I showed mercy, my father would order his slaves to tie me to a post and lash me with a riding crop. The boy sobbed as I picked up a rock and smashed his face.

I rejected this sorrowful echo and focused on the task of keeping Molyneaux at bay, hoping Bangs and Snake could locate the Annihilators.

Surrounded by yelling, distorted faces leering at us, we collided again and clinched up. The ref whipped us with a bar towel and screamed, "Break, you bastards!" The crowd was too whiskey-blitzed at this point, pushing those closest to the ring against the wires and causing more blood to spill. The ref slipped in the gore, cursing at them and us even more.

We broke and I pressed my attack, Molyneaux ducking my right hook. He came in fast and close, pounding my kidney so hard that I knew I'd be pissing blood for a week. Trying to avoid another body shot, I clinched, but he dealt me a wicked right uppercut between my arms that put me back on my heels. Seeing I was off balance, Molyneaux lowered his shoulder and bull-rushed me, serrating my flesh against the wires, which removed a chunk of skin from my shoulder. I roared and delivered a combination of punches—uppercut, hook, straight—landing the last one flush against his nose, blood gushing from his nostrils.

"You have him!" Clemens cheered. "Don't let up!"

Believing him, I charged, but he side-stepped somehow and I crashed into the wires, tangling my arms. I was unable to duck his punch and in the next moment I was on the floor, stars flashing before me.

Then the ref was right in my face, shrieking the count: "One. Two. Thr—"

I started to get back on my feet when Snake and one of the Annihilators—the one who'd wielded the coffee-mill gun—came crashing into and over the wires, knocking down the referee and causing the entire audience inside the Hump to explode with fury and indignation. Rather than go after my Indian friend and the Texas mercenary, the onlookers started slugging one another, smashing bottles against craniums, and soon there was gunfire, though directed at the ceiling—a failed attempt to calm people down. It had the opposite effect, inciting everyone to demolish the place, starting with tables and chairs upended and used as shields and weapons.

On the floor, Snake had the advantage, blade out and straddling the Annihilator. The Texan held Snake's wrist to keep from getting sliced, and with the other hand was trying to get his fingers around my Indian friend's neck. A black-bearded hulk from the crowd, no doubt incensed at the sight of a Paiute on the verge of gutting a white man, pulled a gun, aiming it at Snake. I was on my feet, stumbling toward the back-shooter, but I couldn't make it in time.

There was a pistol blast, but instead of killing the Indian, the man collapsed like a scythed stalk of wheat. Behind him stood Clemens with a smoking Derringer.

A whip snapped, ripping the gun from his hand. A second Annihilator came forward. Fearsome as he was, the mercenary wielding the pike most alarmed me, but I had to deal with the immediate threat. Still dazed, I went running at the Annihilator as he reared his arm back for another lashing. I brought my arms up to shield my face and went to lunge, but slipped in blood and lost my balance. Falling to the ground, I found myself being choked by the Texan. He used his whip as a garotte, wrenching my head so severely I thought he might decapitate me.

That was when I sensed two large, dark-skinned arms intervene, causing my strangler to yelp. The pressure vanished, and as I gasped and coughed for air, I looked up in time to watch Molyneaux lift the Annihilator over his head and throw him several feet over the crowd to crash against a green-felted faro table, shattering it. Molyneaux kept the whip and cracked it at a group of spectators who'd decided to try to climb through the wires for more fisticuffs. They retreated at the sight and sound of the hulking boxer, ready to tear off their faces with a leather scourge.

Snake, meanwhile, was about to plunge his knife into the other Annihilator's neck when the pike came swinging into view. I finally saw him, this pike-wielder—a bow-legged, coyote-faced gullyfluff, grinning like a mad bastard as he hooked Snake by the seat of his buckskins, catapulting him all the way up to the ceiling and letting him crash to the floor.

To his credit, Bangs, the fussy Pinkerton, leaped off a table to tackle the pikeman, slamming him onto his back and getting in wicked licks as the Annihilator curled up to avoid losing consciousness.

I crawled under the wires and got to my feet, intent on helping Bangs, when suddenly the sound of a heavy gun—which I recognized as an M1819 Hall single-shot breech-loading rifle—blasted through the chaos, causing everyone to freeze. The sudden quiet was so thorough and complete, you could hear a bottle rolling on the wooden bar floor until it tinkled against a pile of splintered furniture.

"Molyneaux," a voice snarled from behind a dense cloud of gun smoke. "Stop lashing the whites. Though their services are dubious, we will require them in the coming weeks."

I recognized the sinister timbre, the perverse cadence and odd phrasing. It was a menacing tenor older than time, more deranged than the darkest dreams of men of infinite power and savagery. The voice cut me to the quick and carved my bones and guts with its evil force.

Nursing his whip-raked hand, Clemens broke the silence. "Kid, this man seems familiar. He has a Georgia accent reminiscent of...well, I guess I want to point out that he sounds like you."

The mist of gun smoke dissipated, and the man revealed himself, holding the rifle with one hand and standing with the help of a cane, gold alligator jaws decorating its head. He wore a tailored cotton frock coat the color of burgundy, with a high collar and brass buttons, reflecting both status and refinement. Beneath the coat was a crisp white linen shirt with ruffled cuffs. His waistcoat, intricately patterned, was polished wool, along with his trousers. His leather boots were high-heeled and pointed. His appearance was the paragon of Southern elegance and sophistication, disguising a heart utterly shriveled and blackened by a twisted lust for money and power, for watching people submit to his demented fantasies…and then die.

"This man," I said, wiping blood from my mouth with the back of my hand, "is my father."

"The apple," Clemens replied, "fell very far from the tree."

"Not far or fast enough," my father said, the black boxing champion standing beside him, still holding the whip.

And then, he did something I'd seen only a time or two.

Dear old Dad actually laughed.

11

SHIRTLESS AND BLOODY, I STOOD BESIDE MY battered friends—newspaperman Samuel Clemens, Paiute warrior Snake, Pinkerton Detective Bangs. We squared off against prizewinning pugilist Tom Molyneaux and the most notorious and malevolent plantation owner in the South, also known as Carson Crimson. As he smirked at me and my crew, the Annihilators brushed the dust from their clothes, rubbed their necks, and cracked their knuckles before joining their employer in this standoff. The fight crowd had dissipated, but a few dozen men observed, eager to discover what exactly had happened to ruin the boxing match slated for the night.

"You're looking terrible, Father."

"And you look lean and regal, son. You carry yourself like your mother."

His comment about the woman who bore me pursed my lips, but otherwise I ignored it. "You hired these Texas clowns to do what, exactly?"

He handed his cane to Molyneaux, pulled a gold case from his coat, and fished out a cigarette as one of the

Annihilators, the pikeman, obsequiously extended a match. My father took a long drag. "First," he said, "we reorganize Silver City. Then we build a rail through Devil's Gate. And in a few months, we annex the silver mines of Virginia City."

"The Union army at Fort Churchill might have something to say about that. Your Annihilators and your brawler here are hardly bulletproof."

"Son, you know I relish...collaborations. I'm working under the authority of the governor of the Territory of Nevada to implement this plan. The men of Silver City are done working long, dangerous hours to keep Virginia City pampered and well-paid. It's their turn now."

"Why would Governor Nye authorize you to do anything?"

"The Union needs rail shipments through the West. You forget, son, that I played an important role in constructing the Central Rail Road & Canal Company of Georgia."

I hadn't forgotten. But when he mentioned his experience, something else clicked in my mind like the latch on a jewelry box. To keep Carson Crimson out of Dixie and to stop him from financing Jefferson Davis's Rebels, Lincoln must have had Governor Nye lure him to Nevada to get the railroad up and running. No doubt Nye offered my father a serious percentage of the profits.

"I don't care if Lincoln or God Himself tasked you," I said, head throbbing from my two concussions of the day. "What makes you think I'll allow you to operate in the West?"

"No one cares what you will or won't allow," my father said, raising his whiskey-ravaged voice and spiking my heart rate. "You're outclassed here and there's nothing you and your mild bunch can do to stop us." He pointed the tip of his cane at me, then made a gun-recoil gesture, a threat.

Molyneaux leaned in and muttered something. My father smiled. "I'm reminded, by the by, that we're discontinuing the prohibition against blood sport. Thought you should know."

My rage was growing beyond my control. "And that reminds me that you and your thugs slaughtered the family at the Cisco station, including the young wife and two boys, for no good reason other than your utter despicable vicious—"

"Might makes right is reason enough in these United States, in this day and age, wouldn't you say, boys?"

At that moment, a horde of labor-toughened men gathered around him, the toilers of Silver City—horseshoers, transport drivers, millworkers. In their calloused hands, they carried broken shovels, bottles, and kitchen knives. Angered by my ruse to present myself as a renowned boxer, they glowered, shuffling forward slightly to communicate their growing displeasure.

"No," my father said. "Let them go. There's nothing Kid Crimson can do to halt progress in the West. To take a stand against the railroad is to defy nature itself."

I couldn't help myself now. I shouted, "I defy you, old man, and everything you stand for!"

Clemens reached out and placed his hand on my shoulder. A not-so-subtle nudge for me to retreat.

My father lowered his head, staring at me through narrowed eyes. "Yes. At this time, though, defiance will cost you. I suggest you choose a more opportune moment to fight, son. Have some whiskey for the road."

"As I've liked to say since arriving in Nevada," Clemens chimed in in an effort to distract me, "whiskey is for drinking; water is for fighting over. Kid and I—and, well, his friends here whom I'm eager to learn more about—are going to grab a bottle and be on our way."

"Smart idea," Molyneaux said, "to limit the drama."

"I can't actually guarantee an undramatic exit without the company of a certain female scribe. Her name is Clementine Dunn and I'm afraid we need her back. She has become beloved company in Virginia City and is dearly missed."

"Hank, too," I said, clenching and unclenching my fists, even though they were beaten to a pulp. "The stage driver is my friend and I'm not leaving without him."

Carson Crimson exhaled a plume of smoke, letting silence hang heavy in the room, something he was good at. We listened to the men around him breathing, coughing, belching. He was letting us know that he could, with the snap of his fingers, unleash his tavern dogs on us.

"Wesley," he said finally, calling out to the Annihilator with the whip. "Our guests have stayed with us long enough. It's time they returned home."

Wesley pushed Dunn and Hank, struggling against the rope tying their hands behind them, into the center of the crowd. Clemens caught the frazzled girl before she fell, holding her in his arms as if she might spring to life again and begin dancing. The two writers looked somehow quite dashing and indefatigable together in the weird light of the Hump, surrounded by haunted men of the high desert, silver processors, beast masters, and leathercrafters.

"Samuel," she said, eyes fluttering. "You rescued me." She craned her neck to kiss his lips and he returned the affection.

Hank stumbled toward us, his face bruised. Snake took him by the arm, drew a knife, and cut the stage driver's bonds. Hank rubbed his wrists and looked carefully at the Paiute warrior for a moment before nodding his appreciation.

"We'll take whiskey now," Bangs insisted. "All this fighting has worked up a powerful thirst."

"Whiskey," my father said, "is on the house. Take a few bottles with you for your return through Devil's Gate." Then, to everyone else, he spoke like a professional stage actor. "Our guests here at the Hump are to be left alone and unblemished as they leave Silver City."

And just like that, he turned around and headed up the stairs to what I assumed was his office, Tom Molyneaux and the Annihilators following him.

Finally, inevitably, nearly twenty years of pent-up fury and contempt exploded and barely knowing what I was saying or doing, I roared, "Don't you dare turn your back on me, old man!"

Clemens and Bangs and Snake tried desperately to restrain me, but I was too enraged to be stopped. I went racing toward my father as he ascended the staircase.

Molyneaux turned at the sound of my clomping boots and delivered a vicious punch with a fist like a pickax. The room began spinning fast and I collapsed against an upside down table, a wooden leg gouging my ribs. Consciousness drifted away, just out of reach.

Then darkness swallowed me.

———

I WOKE up in my bed in Virginia City, Poppy stroking my hair and singing a Chinese lullaby. My head was pierced through and through with pain; my hands throbbed from the impact of striking Molyneaux. I hurt so badly that I hesitated to touch my wife, gorgeous as she was.

When she saw me stirring, her lips grazed my cheek and I pulled her in close, wanting to forget the nightmare of having encountered my father in Silver City, a town just four miles from where my family lived. Had I actually survived? Or was this a bitter death?

"Tell me this isn't a dream, or worse," I said. "Tell me I'm alive and lying in bed with you."

"You're alive and in bed with the woman who loves you," Poppy confirmed. "But I have a warning, Kid. If you continue to get your head smashed in, there won't be anything for me to love. Just a pile of broken bones in a casket prepared by Grover." She kissed my ear like a gentle breeze, so softly, with so much feminine affection I was convinced I was in heaven.

"How long?"

"Not long. You arrived in the morning and it's late afternoon now. Dr. Scullard—"

"You didn't let him examine me, did you?"

"I did. He was sober. His diagnosis is 'boxer's plague.' You suffered a seizure on the wagon ride back to Virginia City. He says if you continue in this line of work, you'll end up dead."

"I've heard that particular concern," I said, reaching for a glass of water on the nightstand. "Another good reason to leave for California."

Poppy playfully swatted my hand, came around to the other side of the bed, and brought the glass to my lips. Her belly looked even fuller, more rounded than before. I desired her in that moment, wanting very much to slip her out of her cream-colored, off-shoulder, ruffle-tiered maternity dress and press both her small plum-sized breasts into my mouth.

She sensed my craving and carefully, slowly, hiked her

skirt to straddle me in bed, my body nude under the sheets.

"I think I should let you rest," she said. "I don't want to worsen your condition."

The pain in my skull was intensifying. Still, I used my teeth to pull down the top of her dress. I could taste blood on my knuckle-split lips, but that didn't stop me.

"Kid," Poppy said with concern, "you're bleeding."

Pressing my face into her armpit, I savored her delicious scent. She moaned quietly before saying, "My cousin Sing and the kids are downstairs playing Pai Gow at the kitchen table. We can't make noise or they'll rush right up here."

I chuckled, which caused my ribs to throb. "Sing is teaching them to gamble?"

She looked down at me with a smile, her long raven-black hair falling around me. "They have to learn at some point. This way they'll get bored of it."

"You have an interesting parenting philosophy." I licked her clavicle, which tasted like salt and lemon and clover honey. "Did my friends make it back okay?"

"They did. They're worried and want to meet you at the Blood Nugget tonight. There's a Pinkerton among them, a man named Bangs."

Poppy wore no undergarments and I could feel her pubic hair skim my stomach as she gingerly kissed my chest. Then I felt her moisture. I couldn't tell if I found her more beautiful when pregnant or if I'd missed her terribly in the short time I was gone.

"I'll meet them for dinner in that case. After I feast on you."

It was all bravado and pretense; I couldn't even imagine getting out of bed, let alone spending the evening carousing in a boisterous bar. And desire was one thing, while my body being able to do anything about it was entirely another thing.

This was the worst I'd felt since I couldn't remember when. And not just my aching head, battered hands, and abraded skin. The arrival of Carson Crimson had turned my world upside down and inside out, to the point that I couldn't distinguish between my dizziness from all the recent head banging and the disorientation from the turmoil associated with my father.

Nellie Brown, the knife-throwing circus performer who'd accompanied me to Utah to battle Prince Polignac, had warned me that my father was heading this way, but I didn't take her seriously. After all, it turned out that Polignac was her husband and that was enough of a shock to make everything else insignificant by comparison.

Insignificant is how I felt in the aftermath of the Silver City brawl, physically and spiritually. To come face to face with a man I'd put a bullet into years ago was beyond disturbing. Knowing that Scullard, a drunken doctor but still a physician, believed another blow might kill me felt like a defining nail in the coffin I was building for myself as a gunman in Virginia City.

"Kid," Poppy said, "I need to know something."

"Yes, my flower?"

"Your friends seem, well, shocked by having met your father. Even Snake. You've described him to me before, but I wonder…"

I waited for her to come out with it.

"You don't think he's after our little ones, do you? Ezra and Sarah and our—"

Anger speared me in the guts and pierced my aching noggin. I hadn't considered such a terrifying possibility until Poppy mentioned it. The room started to spin and I fought to maintain what little equilibrium I had left.

"Kid, I'm sorry," she said, still in bed and on her knees, her palms open. "I didn't mean to—"

I held up my hands to slow her down until I could catch up. I squeezed my eyes shut and it took every ounce of energy not to descend into a hole deeper and blacker than the farthest edge of John Mackay's mine. Finally, I resurfaced and opened my eyes—to see my wife staring at me, tears rolling down her cheeks.

"You don't need to apologize, Poppy. I'm the one who's sorry, so sorry to be putting you through all this. Listen, he's a hard bastard to kill, but I've killed tougher. I was only nineteen when I shot him and made the rookie mistake of not finishing him off. But I promise you this. My father will never touch our children. Or you. I'll kill him and everyone around him if he tries."

"I feel terrible, like I summoned him here," she sobbed. She wiped her eyes with the back of her hands, then moved her beautiful hair from her face, placing it behind her ears.

"How could you have summoned him?"

"I don't know. Maybe he sensed your happiness somehow and felt compelled to show up and destroy us. You always said he was supernaturally diabolical."

I thought that over, my head pounding like the bass drum in a marching band. She was right, of course. I had said that and I believed it. But rather than riling her up even more than she was, I said, "Poppy, he's lived like a dog and he'll die like a dog."

"Let's leave Virginia City now, Kid. We don't have to stay. I'll sell the opium house to Ralston."

"I'd like nothing more, believe me. But what if he follows us to California? We can't keep trying to outrun him. That will just encourage him. Best to deal with him here, where I have friends and allies."

It was then that I noticed what was mounted on the wall above the headboard—Poppy's rifle.

She noticed me noticing. "A precaution is all. I'm not worried if you're not."

"Oh, I'm worried, and you should be too."

"About Carson Crimson coming here?"

I shook my head. "About what I plan to do to stop him."

"I've long worried about that," Poppy said, using the bedsheet to dab the last tear from her eye.

———

I COULDN'T JOIN my crew for dinner at the Blood Nugget. So they came to the house on B Street. I hated for them to see me infirm, but in my present condition, there was no way I could risk some miscreant with a grudge bashing me over the head with a bottle or an Annihilator sent to do the job. Actually, I didn't want to see anyone, but they insisted. Poppy and Sing took the kids on an excursion to her cousin's pig ranch and the six of us—Bangs, Clemens, Snake, Dunn, and myself—gathered in the drawing room. Despite suffering a few bruises from our Silver City hijinks, Hank Monk was already working a route toward Colorado, a job done for, I suspected, Ralston. I needed to chat with Ralston about my father soon, and I wasn't looking forward to it. Lennox, meanwhile, had taken a shine to the soprano, who was also under the care of Dr. Scullard. Lennox was visiting her in her room in the Gold Hill Hotel, where the boxer Con Orem was also recovering. Our gathering was a somber affair, with no whiskey and all of us resigned to defeat. Well, except for Bangs who wore a defiant expression.

"Your father," he growled, "killed my partner."

"My father has killed a lot of people and there will be even more."

"You mentioned having shot him," Clemens said. "Seems you missed a vital organ."

"I don't know," I said. "Truth be told, I rarely miss. So far in his miserable life, he's been impossible to kill."

Everyone shared a look when I refused to elaborate.

"Where do we go from here, Tiny?" Snake asked. "Your father seduced the whole town of Silver City, seems like. We can't fight a thousand men to reach him."

Bangs looked around before saying, "We could snuff Daddy Crimson and his Annihilators in a nighttime raid. But we need Lennox and as many hard cases as Kid can muster."

"I can bring any number of violent lunatics to Silver City," I said. "What I need to figure out is who is funding my father. Governor Nye can't be letting him rob stage-coaches."

"Clearly he's operating in Silver City without drawing the wrath of the US Army," Bangs said.

"Carson Crimson," Dunn said, pushing up her glasses, "is a mystery. Is he well known in the South?"

Bangs scoffed. "He's absolutely notorious for being a brutal plantation owner. He's killed many politicians and corrupted many women in a bid for power throughout the South and Washington before…well, before the schism." He looked at me for a second, then settled his gaze on Poppy's Winchester displayed on the wall. "Sorry, Kid. I'm just relating—"

"No apology necessary."

"I have orders," the Pinkerton went on, "to keep the

stages running and to rid the area of any Confederate influences."

"Confederate?" Dunn asked. "Hang on. How do we know Carson Crimson is telling the truth about working for Governor Nye?"

"She's right. My father is the prince of lies," I said. "Nye's authorization is something Clemens can confirm through his brother Orion, the Secretary of Nevada."

"That I can do. But Kid, I hope you don't mind me pointing it out."

"What's that?"

"Your father likely has another motive besides insinuating himself into elite circles in the West."

"You don't have to say it."

"Say what, exactly?" Dunn apparently couldn't help herself from wondering out loud.

"He's here to kill me and everyone I love."

"If that's true," Snake said, "and that's a big if, Kid—"

Snake was interrupted by the front door being flung open and hitting the wall, then Ezra sprinting in, panting like a dog. "Grover's place! It's on fire!"

Everyone at the table, myself not included, jumped to their feet and hurried out the front door.

Dunn hung back. "Aren't you coming, Kid?

"In due time. I'm not running and I'm not fighting a fire, not even at Grover's."

"Isn't there a fire department?"

"Yes. But they spend most of their time drinking and gambling."

She knew about my relationship with the town undertaker. As we went out the back to the horses, she said, "Think he was targeted?"

I saddled up my Appaloosa for the short ride to Grover's, indicating to the dime novelist that she should join me. "I'll find out. Sure my father's men didn't harm you?"

She said nothing at first. Instead, she grabbed the reins of my animal and brought us over to a barrel so that she could step up more easily and slide in behind me.

"No one hurt me," she finally said, as my horse took off toward Sun Mountain.

"Can I ask you a question now, Kid?"

"Sure."

"When you finally kill your father, will it bring you peace?"

I almost slapped the reins to gather speed, but thought better of it. I had just enough energy to answer her. "There's no peace in this world."

12

—————

THE AIR WAS THICK WITH ACRID SMOKE AS AN ominous glow flickered near the base of the mountain. It was obvious, even at a distance, that the mortuary couldn't be saved and I was too weary, in pain, and somber to even pretend I could help. As Dunn and I trotted Grover's, I had time to pray that my surrogate father wasn't at his place when my real father, I strongly suspected, had it torched.

When we reached the blaze, the structure was engulfed, flames licking hungrily at snapping hardwood beams. The devastation was fueled by parched wood and fanned by relentless desert winds. Stunned onlookers— mostly Chinese and Indians—stared in disbelief as the sanctuary for the departed became a crucible for destruction. It was nearing twilight, the fire painting the sky a hellish palette. The faint, cloying perfume of embalming fluid and the tang of kerosene soured the smoky breeze. We heard Grover's glass containers exploding from the intense heat, along with the splintering crash of collapsing timber.

Inside the office, cherished memories turned to ash, including Grover's photography—tintypes of me in an air balloon, of him and me standing beside Lincoln's body double at the railroad station, of Hannibal the armored war elephant charging Prince Polignac's French mercenaries. The satin-lined coffin I slept in between arriving in Virginia City and getting married was likely incinerated, along with the gifts I'd given him over the years—a King James Bible, an engraved Starr Arms Co. model 1863 revolver, a brass nautical sundial ripped from the captain's cabin of a whaling ship in Nantucket. These were mere objects, yet they were tokens of my deep affection for the man who took me in when I showed up to Virginia City, haggard and beaten from fighting the Paiute at Pyramid Lake days after trekking to Nevada from Georgia. Grover had saved me, and every gift I bestowed him was a symbol of my immense love for him.

To my relief, Grover wasn't wounded or even ruffled by the fire. He'd been chewing on a steak at the Blood Nugget when it erupted, but who or what caused it was something I needed to figure out. At the moment, he was engaged with the volunteer bucket brigade—an informal band of degenerate drinkers hoping for free whiskey from the saloons in exchange for their minimal response to fires. The men hooted like escaped maniacs, uselessly splashing one another with water from a nearby well. Eventually, they formed a double line, one line filling buckets, passing them up to the fire, where water was thrown at the burning structure. Empty buckets were quickly passed back, via the second line of people, to be refilled in the well. My friends, meanwhile, had shown up with the more serious firemen who handled the town's steam-driven ladder truck, a boiler tank primed to saturate everything in sight.

"The odor of kerosene is strong," Dunn said, sliding daintily off the back of my saddle as I pulled the reins. "This was no accident, Kid."

She was right. The roof was caved in, wrecked by a projectile. Bright-orange flames suggested an accelerant. Dunn had her notepad out, writing down everything she saw. I was grateful for this. Groggy from the punishment I'd endured, I needed someone to confirm the many clues.

I was about to dismount when I spotted a dust cloud near the summit of Mount Davidson. I retrieved my field glasses to get a better look.

"Up on the mountain," I said.

"What do you see?" Dunn said.

"Men on horses. They've got something with them."

"What is it?"

Dark-clothed outlaws followed alongside a wheeled contraption, navigating the trail that ran along the peak. Sunlight fading, I made out the silhouettes of men, one of them moving similarly to Wesley the whip-cracker, an Annihilator. The war machine they towed was a monstrous creation of wood and iron, pulled by sturdy draft horses. It towered majestically, an odd and massive blend of ancient warfare and frontier technology.

Then the weapon—and men accompanying it—disappeared over the mountain, vanishing like a sinister mirage. Even if I were fully healed, I couldn't have chased them down. Besides, everything had the strangeness of a dream. I wasn't sure if what I'd seen was real or imaginary.

"Kid, talk to me."

I put away the field glasses and considered Grover's office, a conflagrated ruin. The splashing inebriates had already dropped their buckets on the ground and given up, bent over and coughing from all the fumes they'd inhaled. The ladder company, meanwhile, had just figured out that the blaze was oil-based and had more success with throwing sand on the flames.

"It seems that the Annihilators launched a kerosene barrel into Grover's funeral home."

"With what?"

"A trebuchet."

"Excuse me?"

"A catapult with a sling attached to the arm. A stone-throwing siege engine."

"Your father used a medieval weapon to destroy your friend's business."

I nodded. "Probably testing it out, with the intent of building more—"

"Trebuchets," Dunn finished my sentence.

"My father," I went on, "possesses a violent and diabolical mind. Growing up on his plantation, I'm privy to his strange predilections." I finally dismounted.

The dime novelist jotted down my statement, folded her notepad, and tucked it into the pocket of her velvet coat. She placed the pencil between her teeth, then walked over and patted my horse. She studied me and removed the pencil to say, "You don't look well."

"I'm not well. Carson Crimson plans to take over Virginia City and is gunning for my family."

"That's not what I meant. You're pale, hunched over, and your eyes are sunken."

The wind shifted, a pall of smoke falling on us. We stepped backward to escape the flurry of soot.

"All I need's a good night's sleep.

"And then what?"

"And then I kill my father. Again."

"How do you intend to do that?"

"First, I need to interview the magician." The fire had sputtered out, leaving a smoldering ruin, and I saw Grover, his clothes soaked and stained, making his way over.

"Magician?" Dunn said.

"Thurston Larue."

"Ah, yes," Dunn used her pencil to put her gorgeous hair in a bun. "President Lincoln's favorite conjurer. I saw a handbill announcing Larue's performance in the opera house tomorrow."

"I was looking for him when we ended up rescuing the boxer and the soprano, Nora Pearl. She claims Larue was on the stagecoach with her and Con Orem. Curious that the magician wasn't also thrown into the hole, no?"

"Right," Dunn said. "Bangs mentioned the Annihilators took Larue. They seemed familiar with one another."

I wanted to ask her if she'd known Bangs prior to Virginia City. Grover, however, had reached us, exhausted but also relieved to see me. We embraced tightly, and he cleared the smoke from his throat. I sensed he was unsure about Dunn.

"The Pinkerton," he said, "insists your father did this. He's alive, apparently."

Shame and anger reddened my face. "Grover, I'm sorry."

He waved away my culpability. "I'm lucky, Kid. I'm usually in bed at this hour and could've easily been asleep in the office. Anyhow, I'm insured, thanks to Ralston. I'm relieved you made it back from Silver City."

"I'm thankful you decided to enjoy a late dinner."

"Kid," Grover said, voice quiet and low. "I observed a fascinating character lurking in the Blood Nugget. A man who boasted of being an escape artist."

Dunn and I looked at each other.

"Speaking of the devil. Did he happen to call himself the Shadow Man?"

Grover nodded. "Thurston Larue. We didn't meet. He chatted with the miners and bar girls. Unless he showed up here to watch my coffins burn, I'd wager he's still at the bar."

Dunn extended her hand to Grover. "I'm Clementine Dunn, by the way."

Grover smiled and shook. "Ah. The writer from New York. We here in Virginia City love the adventures you've penned about our hometown hero." He mock bowed in front of me.

"Well, I've only been in town a few days," she said, "and I have plenty more to write."

"By the time you leave, you'll have volumes."

Listening to them talk about me while I stood there was uncomfortable. Or maybe my pounding headache and blurred vision was making me paranoid and disagreeable. "I'll check on our visiting entertainer at the Blood Nugget."

"I'll tag along, Kid," Dunn said. "Wonderful to meet you, Grover."

He offered a weary salute, then wiped his sweaty brow with the sleeve of his grimy shirt. "The feeling's mutual. You know, I could honestly use your help, Miss Dunn, with new advertising language in the *Territorial Enterprise*. My storage shed is unscathed, and I should let people know I can still care for their dearly departed."

"Of course," she said. "Tomorrow morning, ten o'clock?"

"Perfect. See you then, ma'am."

I saddled up my Appaloosa and Dunn slid in behind

me. "Given thought to Bangs's plan to launch a night-time attack on your father?"

"I have, but I like my plan better." My horse neighed as I slapped the reins.

"Which is what?"

"Befriend the magician and learn secrets."

"Secrets?"

"About my father's conspiracy and how to foil it."

"Don't you know your father's methods by now?"

"Yes," I said. "But his madness can be unpredictable."

Dunn was quiet for several moments. Finally, she spoke. "I lied, Kid."

I didn't say anything, waiting.

I felt her arms wrapped around me, her hands on my chest. I felt her press her lovely forehead between my shoulder blades. "Your father hurt me, and I don't ever want to talk about it."

I stopped my horse and gazed straight ahead at the lights of Virginia City's C Street. I clenched my jaw as I imagined eviscerating my father with a jagged shard of glass.

"I'll kill him, Clementine," I said. "And this time I won't fail."

She emitted a muffled sob. "I hope so."

———

THE LAST THING I felt like doing was walking into the Blood Nugget to trade wits with a magician. But if I didn't, I'd probably miss my opportunity. When Dunn and I entered, arm in arm, it caused Chaparral, my friend the piano player, to raise an eyebrow. What he didn't know was that we were lending each other physical and moral support. He went back to pounding out "Battle

Cry of Freedom," inciting the Irish miners to howl the melody and words with abandon, hanging onto one another with sloppy, brotherly fondness.

Perched on a stool at the bar, Thurston Larue drank whiskey and flirted with a saloon girl I knew. Clad in a tailored black frock coat with intricate silver embroidery, he exuded an air of mystery. His crisp white shirt was a contrast against the coat, accentuating the gleam in his eyes. A yellow silk cravat cascaded elegantly down his chest, drawing attention to a pocket watch with an ornate chain dangling from his waistcoat. His trousers were charcoal, tailored to perfection, tapering into polished leather boots. Every detail of his attire spoke of elegance and a touch of otherworldly charm. He pulled her close and placed his lips near her ear, uttering something that made her giggle.

Still smiling, she was about to reply, until she saw Dunn and me. Her face went serious, waiting for instruction. I indicated she should work the other side of the bar and she immediately picked up her drink and sashayed away.

Larue reached for her arm, but I was already standing next to him.

"I recognize you," I said. "You're the man on the poster."

"Yes," he said, frowning and frustrated to have lost his female companion, still watching her as she sat at another table of whiskey-ripped miners. "I'm famous to a degree."

"A large degree," I said. "Don't be modest. My wife and I enjoyed your show in Silver City."

"A town of hard-drinkers, but a delightful audience. Except for the gentleman who threatened to stew the rabbit I pulled from a hat."

"Yes, well, there's an attention-seeker in every crowd. You know, I consider myself a bit of a magician."

"Really," he said, sipping his beer and completely uninterested.

"I've been perfecting a trick. It's called the Spirit Coffin."

Now I had his attention. He turned to assess me, starting with my clothes. "You certainly don't fit the physical mold of a trickster. What did you say your name was?"

I opened my mouth to speak, but my fist-bashed mind couldn't improvise a fictional name.

"My husband's name," said Clementine, saving me, "is Deacon Dunn. My name is Clementine."

She presented her hand, Larue smirking as he gently kissed it and said, "Charmed, Mrs. Dunn."

"Want to see my magic trick?" I said, producing from my coat the Spirit Coffin Grover had given me days earlier.

Larue opened his palms, suggesting he wished to hold it. "May I?"

I placed it in his hands and he examined it, opening the lid to find the piece of white chalk inside. He returned it to me without saying anything.

"Ready?"

"I am."

I asked the bartender, my good friend Jericho, for paper and pencil, then slid the items over to Larue. "Write down the name of the scariest person you know."

"Historical or current?"

"Current."

He wrote down the name, folded the paper twice, and placed it beneath his empty beer glass.

I closed the Spirit Coffin. It was still quite noisy

thanks to Chaparral's piano, so I gestured to him to lower the volume and he obliged. Then Larue, Clementine, and I leaned in, listening for the sound of chalk moving around inside the miniature wooden coffin.

There was a squeak and some scratching noises.

Larue laughed. "A yummy deception."

The Spirit Coffin ceased rattling. I picked it up and opened it, the lid facing Larue.

"What does it say?"

"This," he said, reaching for the paper, which he opened so that I could read the name: Carson.

I turned the Spirit Coffin to see that the names indeed matched.

"Not too shabby, Mr. Dunn." He shook my hand firmly. "Pleasure to meet a fellow mage."

"I'm flattered."

"You've made his night," Clementine said. "Maybe his whole life."

"Don't let it go to your head. It's one thing to present a magic act to an audience of one. It's quite another to pull it off expertly in front of hundreds."

"My husband enjoys an audience. He loves it when others watch."

Intrigued, Larue grinned at her mischievously.

"This Carson," I said, "must be pretty diabolical to unnerve an illusionist of your caliber."

"Oh, I'm not frightened of what he'll do to me. I'm not his target. He has...a city to conquer."

"Well, he sounds intimidating. I'm glad he doesn't reside here in Virginia City."

Larue snapped his fingers, ordering another beer for himself and whiskey for Clementine and me. A true professional, Jericho already had the drinks poured and slid them down the bar. Clementine took a ladylike sip while I pretended to drink. When Larue turned to guzzle his beer and I was sure he wasn't spying on me, I discreetly dumped the whiskey on the floor. He slammed his half-full mug on the bar top, wiped his mouth with the sleeve of his frock, and said, "No, but he arrives tomorrow, actually. He's attending my performance. This is, after all, the city he plans to conquer."

13

IN THE MORNING, I HAD BREAKFAST WITH Ralston at the Griddle of Doom. Appetite dulled by the continuing pain in my head and below, the emotional impact of last night's arson, and the strain of my father attending Larue's performance that night in Virginia City, I couldn't bring myself to touch the stack of syrup-drenched chocolate chip pancakes Ralston had ordered for me. I considered pushing the plate toward him so he could wolf down my food too.

"Sending you through Devil's Gate without a bigger team wasn't my best idea," he said, biting into his waffle coated in powdered sugar, unfazed by my lack of hunger.

I shrugged. "Well, we recovered the passengers... except for the magician who has a show tonight at the opera house. Your investment bonds are gone, I'm afraid."

"Chat with Larue?"

"I did, last night at the Blood Nugget."

"He spoke with you...willingly?"

"Not with me, exactly. I presented myself as a fellow magician."

Ralston chuckled at this. "And what did he reveal?"

"That my father will be coming up from Silver City to see the show."

Ralston put down his fork and knife and stared. "You'll arrest him, I assume. Put him in jail on charges."

"I'm not a sheriff."

"I can fix that."

"What would I charge him with? He claims Governor Nye is his boss."

Ralston took a sip of coffee. "That part is true. What's false is your father's authorization to rob stagecoaches."

And murder innocents, I thought, but kept it to myself. "Why can't the Army dislodge him from Silver City?"

"Besides Nye's ignorance and power hunger? Basically that the Army is busy slaughtering Indians, who stand in the way of progress."

As much as I appreciated Ralston's jobs and his money, I sometimes repressed the urge to strangle him when he spoke glibly about killing for the sake of westward expansion. "Still," I said, "I can't figure out the magician's role."

"He's an escape artist. An illusionist. Perhaps he's here to bust someone out of jail."

"We don't have a jail."

"Not here, but maybe Fort Churchill."

"I don't understand."

Ralston sighed, wiped his beard with a napkin. "A number of Confederate sympathizers are awaiting trial there for insurrection. You mentioned months ago that your father remains a member of the Knights of the Golden Circle."

"I guess it's possible," I said. "But my father isn't known for rescuing anyone, even Rebels. Who do they have locked up at Fort Churchill?"

"The name George Bickley mean anything to you?"

Of course it did. Bickley, a physician from Virginia, had created the Knights of the Golden Circle after being hounded by creditors. He convinced financiers in Texas to support his invasion of Mexico—only he didn't show up with nearly enough mercenaries. The most effective thing the Golden Circle accomplished was blowing up a pro-Union newspaper office in San Antonio. He'd been arrested a year later in Indiana as a Confederate spy.

More significantly to me, personally, Bickley was among the men who'd promoted the child-fighting circuit in Georgia. At nine years old, I'd watched him bet on the blood sport, laughing and drinking and smoking cigars as my fellow kid-brawlers and I hurt one another in pits. We bled and wept and died of infection as he and other elites did nothing to help us, as he and other unconscionable men lost and won money based on the outcome of the savagery we inflicted and suffered. I didn't know Bickley had been transferred to face a tribunal in the Territory of Nevada and I had to wonder why.

"You think my father has dispatched a magician to break Bickley out of Fort Churchill?"

"I don't know for sure, but it seems within the realm of possibility."

"You realize Larue is Lincoln's favorite spellcaster."

"Yes, but it's notable that as a soldier, Larue boasted of willingly being imprisoned by Rebels so he could escape their death camps."

I had similar questions. Had Larue allowed himself to be captured in order to share information with the

Confederates? Was his medical discharge from the Union army legitimate?

"A bold conspiracy, if real," I said. "My father invades Virginia City, stopping silver processing, while breaking the leader of the Knights of the Golden Circle out of a military prison."

Ralston summoned the waiter to clear our plates. "Then there's the issue of the trebuchet. You're sure that's what you saw?"

"I'd only seen drawings of it in books that my mother gave me as a kid. But that's what it looked like."

At this point in our conversation, my nose started bleeding. I dabbed it with a napkin.

Changing direction, Ralston said, "Poppy came to see me last night."

Under ordinary circumstances, this would have displeased me. I didn't want her to deal with Ralston without my presence. But I was just too damaged to react. "Are you going to buy her out?"

He took a breath. "The Sure Cure is a licensed business. And profitable. I don't fancy being in the opium business, but I'm sure I can interest certain parties in taking it off her hands. Which I'm happy to do. It's the right time for you and Poppy to...to move forward."

"What are you really saying?"

"What I'm saying is, a hired gun and an opium seller aren't ideal occupations for...for parents."

It was my first smile in days, maybe weeks. "I've long agreed with this view, which is why I've spent close to three years now saving money to buy a grapefruit orchard."

"You won't have to spend any money, Kid. I've purchased the perfect farm for you in Sonoma County.

Think of it as a gratuity for your success in protecting Virginia City."

I was speechless. I didn't know how to respond or even what to think about what I'd just heard. Again, it felt like I was living in a dream. Buying me a farm was the last thing I expected Ralston, or anyone, to do. Yet, on the other hand, it also occurred to me that he probably had ulterior motives for pushing me out of town

"I'm touched, honestly, and grateful. But why would you do such a thing?"

"I'm encouraging you, Kid, to embrace the future you've planned for your family. Your father's appearance in Nevada is, I think, a sign."

"Sign for what?

"That it's time to spare yourself the risk that goes with being Virginia City's defender."

"So you want me to leave immediately? With my family in tow?"

Ralston shook his head. "I need you to save our mining boomtown one last time, Kid."

"It may require killing my father and many of his followers."

"I'll help you accomplish that, Kid. And then your responsibilities to me are complete."

"I won't owe you anything more?"

"Nothing. You'll be free."

I watched him take another sip of coffee. "I've never known the feeling."

"Of freedom?"

"Of embracing the future."

Ralston pondered this. "The present is always ugly and dim and dispiriting. The future is bright and shiny and promising."

An explosion boomed from Ophir Hill, another hole in the mountain gouged by gunpowder.

"I hope to one day live in the future."

"Me, too, Kid."

———

ANOTHER EXPLOSION EMANATED from the area near Uncle John John's farm at the base of the mountain, nowhere near the mining shafts of the Comstock. If the looks on the faces of the other people at the Griddle of Doom were any indication, it sounded unusual to everyone who heard it. I recognized immediately that something was wrong, and I had an awful feeling that someone I loved was in terrible danger.

Not only couldn't I shake the feeling on my short walk home, but it grew even stronger. When I arrived at the house to check on the kids, Ezra was standing on the front porch, panting and with tears in his eyes.

"Sarah is tending the hogs at Uncle John John's," he said frantically

I still wasn't thinking straight. Ezra, who knew how to read every expression on my face, even the most microscopic, yelled, "Didn't you hear the explosion? That's where it came from!"

"Hop on."

I reached down to hoist him onto the horse, but I didn't expect him to swing himself in front of me and commandeer the reins. I had to hang on for dear life as he urged the Appaloosa, faster and faster toward the billowing smoke emanating from the farmhouse. It only took us a few minutes to reach the property, debris scattered like confetti in a storm. A projectile, what looked like a flaming barrel again, had punched through a corner of the roof, a jagged breach exposing the fiery interior. Glass shards from shattered windows glittered on the ground, the front porch splintered and collapsed under the force of impact.

Ezra and I covered our faces with bandannas from my saddlebag and went inside. The scene was appalling. The kitchen, where Sarah and John John had cooked dumplings and mushroom noodles, was shredded and charred. Shelves that held preserves and dried herbs now sagged precariously, their contents spilled and shattered. A cast-iron stove lay twisted and overturned, its pipes scattered like discarded limbs. Sunlight streamed through the hole in the ceiling, the wooden dining table good now for only kindling. Precious belongings—quilts, photographs—lay strewn about, covered by dirt.

"She's not here," I said. "Let's check outside."

The garden too, bore scars of impact. Tangled vines of squash lay trampled and eaten, pigs from the adjacent pen loose and eating the remnants, but none of the animals appeared to be injured.

Uncle John John calmly walked over from the outhouse, a folded copy of the *Territorial Enterprise* tucked under his armpit. "I went to do a chuanwei and look what happened!"

I couldn't resist. "Saved by the bowels."

"Kid! She's up there!" Desperation gripped Ezra's voice.

"What?" I grabbed my field glasses to scan the rim of the mountain.

Sure enough, the trebuchet was back again, rolling its way over the mountain, surrounded by men on horses. This time though, on the other end of the trail was another dust cloud. I could make out Snake and Bangs atop their sorrels, en route to intercept, just as we'd planned. There was one unanticipated problem, however.

Sarah was on horseback too, incensed by having been fired upon while tending the hogs on John John's farm and racing toward an impending collision between my friends and what I assumed were the Annihilators, evil mercenaries with a lust for murder and who knew what other havoc.

I hesitated. Of course I knew where my duty lay, but I could barely imagine riding up the mountain, let alone engage a bunch of fiends in a battle to the death when I got there. In my indecision, I turned to John John. "Sure you're okay?"

He shooed me away. "My brothers will help me with this mess. Get the girl off that mountain!"

"Sarah," Ezra said, eyes moist with worry, "tends to make a bad situation worse."

"Yes," I said, "it's why we love her."

"I hope she doesn't get killed. She promised to marry me!"

That was news to me. I just looked at him.

He frowned and lowered his head. "Kids at school say you can't marry your sister."

"Sarah isn't your blood relation."

"That's what I told them!"

"Why are you in such a hurry to get married?"

"Because I'm always hungry and wives cook meals for their husbands."

"Good enough. She might be a suffragette though. That type avoids the kitchen."

"Then I'll learn how to cook."

"Better count on that."

My horse snorted with exertion, her muscles rippling beneath the strain of the steep and rapid ascent.

Squinting against the glare of the sun, I heard the distant crack of gunfire echoing through the canyon. A running gun battle was underway. I desperately wanted to stay as far away from it as possible, but at the same time I knew I'd have to wade knee deep in it to get Sarah to turn around and head back to Virginia City.

As her dust cloud came into view, I breathed a sigh of relief. But then I noticed the coyote-faced Annihilator with the pike standing up from behind a boulder that loomed above the entrance to an old mining cavern, its mouth yawning open amid a cliff face.

"Kid," Ezra said, arms wrapped tightly around me. "Who is that?"

"A dead man."

I urged my horse onward, my grip firm on the reins as we navigated a switchback. I gritted my teeth, heart pounding in rhythm with thundering hoofbeats. I raised my gun, taking aim.

"Sarah, get down!" I called out.

She was so lethal, I often forgot that she was only twelve years old. She dropped to the side of her galloping horse, hanging with one heel over the back and one arm looped in a braided sling on the mane while firing a Derringer pistol at the Annihilator she'd already spotted. Her two bullets struck the boulder the mercenary was using for cover, causing him to retreat slightly.

Refusing to let him take a shot at her in the open, she directed her mount into the dark cavern.

Meanwhile, the Annihilator noticed us coming at him fast and swiveled his weapon in our direction.

I thought I had the shot, but my head was pounding, my vision was fuzzy, and my body still ached from the beating I'd taken in Silver City. I squeezed the trigger, the bullet several inches off target. What should've been a headshot struck nothing but sky. Having counted on a bullseye, I didn't slow the horse in time.

The pike swooped and hooked Ezra by his overalls, the Annihilator laughing maniacally. I reached up to yank the boy back into the saddle, but lost my balance and fell.

My body struck the ground and I tasted bitter dust before blacking out.

14

PRONE ON THE GROUND WITH DIRT IN MY mouth, I coughed once. The air was cool and thick with the scent of damp earth and minerals—a contrast to the sour smoke and dust of the chase. I actually felt comfortable for a change. I opened my eyes, which took a few moments to adjust. I was in the embrace of the cavern. I instinctively checked my skull for blood, wet or sticky, and finding none took another moment to get my bearings, scanning the dimly lit tunnel.

"How did I end up here?" I wondered aloud.

To my surprise, Sarah answered. "We dragged you."

"With Buzzard's help."

I let my breath out slowly. Both Ezra and Sarah were safe, at least for the time being.

"Buzzard?"

"Yes sir." The voice came from behind me. "You were gentle with me a few weeks back at the Blood Nugget when I was worried about my brother. I was and am grateful for your kindness."

The memory was vague, but it started to come into view. "Oh. Right. Your brother is Gentry, the whiskey trader Hank Monk and I ran into at the Cisco station."

Sarah lit a lantern. "He was working in this shaft when I came crashing into his rocker box."

"And he saved me," Ezra said. "He shot the pike from the bad guy's hands and I got loose."

"Well, Buzzard, now it's my turn to thank you. I'd say we're even."

"More than happy to oblige, Kid. Much rather be on your good side. 'Sides, these here are a couple of fine young'uns."

I sat up slowly and found, to my surprise, I wasn't too dizzy. I hurt all over, but I was sure I could move without winding up in the dirt again. "Either of you hurt?"

"No, but you took a spill."

"I'm fine," I lied. I felt like someone had reassembled my skeleton using barbed wire.

Buzzard came into my line of sight, framed by sunlight spilling from the mouth of the cavern. I saw that he was carrying a pistol. "We need to move, Kid."

"How many?"

"Three," he said, helping me to my feet.

Using Buzzard's shoulder for support, I found my balance. "Where's my gun?"

"Must've fallen out of your holster," Ezra said.

My brain was scrambled like an egg, my back was against a cavern wall with the Annihilators bearing down on us, and my gun was gone.

"Here," Buzzard said, handing me a sorry single-shot percussion cap. At least he'd reloaded it.

Suddenly there was a hideous scraping sound, sparks flickering wildly at the tunnel opening as the iron pike raked the cavern walls. The nightmare trio strutted confidently toward us, the one named Wesley cracking his slave whip and giggling with sinister malevolence.

I peered into the guts of the cavern, which stretched deeper into the mountain, its walls rough-hewn and humid with moisture seeping through cracks. "Let's go," I said grimly, stumbling on my first few steps amid the rocky miner's path.

I could tell Sarah wanted to stand and fight. "What about our horses?" The two lathered animals were snorting at the ground, hoping for some hay.

"We'll take them as far as we can."

"I'll lead them," Buzzard said, taking the reins in each hand, the stalactites too low to risk us mounting up and cutting our heads.

We pushed deeper into the mine, our footsteps echoing softly against the stone. The air grew colder as we descended. The main tunnel narrowed as smaller passages appeared on all sides. My senses were dulled by the clobbering I'd suffered, but I still heard every creak and drip.

A distant rumble reverberated through the shaft, followed by the sound of voices growing nearer. I cursed softly, pushing Ezra ahead. In turn, he urged Sarah to hurry deeper into the darkness. With the Annihilators on our trail, our only chance lay in finding a way out of this pit before we were backed up against the end wall.

We rounded a corner and I tripped on an old mining cart track, rusted and weed-festooned, wrenching my back as I twisted to keep my balance. But maybe we were getting somewhere. The ceiling was higher at this point, so without hesitation Buzzard and I mounted the horses and pulled the kids up to ride behind us, following the track at a canter. The sounds of pursuit grew louder behind us, the squeaking of wheels and rubber spiking my hackles.

"Buzzard, what's that noise?"

"I don't know, but they're gaining on us."

We urged our mounts to pick up speed, the tunnel we'd chosen seemingly endless, twisting and turning unpredictably as we raced deeper into the mountain's depths.

Hope was fading until Ezra spotted a glimmer of daylight ahead—a tiny opening in the tunnel wall, barely wide enough to squeeze Sarah through.

"It's not big enough for us to escape!" she exclaimed.

"Stand back, everyone," I said, raising the pistol Buzzard lent me.

"No! You'll cave it in on us," he said. "Let me try."

With Sarah sharing the saddle, Buzzard smacked her horse forward with the reins, the animal's hooves pounding against the rough track. With a burst of speed, they smashed through the opening, scattering rocks and dirt clods and clomping into the blinding sunlight.

Ezra and I followed, emerging onto a ledge overlooking a steep ravine, the mountain dropping away sharply beneath us. We scanned our surroundings—the rugged landscape was dotted with scrub brush and sparse trees. Nonetheless, it was a beautiful sight compared to the tunnel's claustrophobic darkness.

"We're not out of this," I said.

Ezra dismounted and sprinted to the tunnel exit, trying to pinpoint our pursuers. "They're coming!"

"We'll use those trees for cover." I pointed to a cluster of stunted pines growing along the edge of the ravine.

Buzzard nodded. "It'll buy us time."

On my horse, nausea suddenly gripped me, and I wasn't sure I could make it. "If I fall again, don't pick me up."

"No whining!" Sarah yelled at me.

Buzzard laughed, music to my ears under the circumstances. "This Indian girl is fiercer than you are, Kid."

We led the horses carefully down a rocky slope toward the trees. I'd navigated rugged terrain before, pursued by Indians and slave-hunters and straight-up killers—but never Annihilators, easily the most lethal outfit I'd ever encountered. Every nerve in my body was on edge for signs of danger, but the beatings dulled my reaction time.

Just as we reached the trees, a gunshot rang out, followed by a wicked laugh. Ezra hit the dirt instinctively.

"Don't stop!" Buzzard commanded.

I looked behind us to see our three pursuers, dressed in dark coats and trousers, weapons in hand, each balancing on what looked like a unicycle. They pedaled to the slope and, maintaining their stability, glided down the path, bouncing on padded seats only slightly as their rubber tires struck a rock or divot. I'd never seen anything so eerie as murderers on one-wheeled, pedal-powered vehicles riding downhill along a mountain path.

"Clever bastards," I said, stopping my horse and drawing a bead with my one-shot.

Before I could fire, a group of five Paiute warriors emerged from the scrub, faces marked with war paint and rifles trained on the Annihilators. One of the Indians was my buddy Snake, but he didn't acknowledge me, glaring at the trinity of murderous Texans.

Buzzard and Ezra and Sarah and I were about to be caught in a crossfire.

I saw Buzzard weighing his choices, mind racing for a way out of this deadly predicament. He didn't realize that the Paiute weren't interested in us. They wanted the Annihilators.

"We mean no harm!" Buzzard called out in godawful Paiute, holding his hands up in a gesture of peace. It was the same gesture settlers at Pyramid Lake had given Snake before he pin cushioned them with arrows.

Meanwhile, the warriors exchanged glances with Snake, their expressions tense with bloodlust. Snake, with braided hair and shirtless, muscles glistening with sweat, moved forward, eyes narrowing as he regarded the Annihilators wheeling toward our position.

"Tiny, your latest friend is goofy," he said, voice rough with authority.

I swallowed hard, searching for the right words to defuse the situation. "Snake, I'm happy you're here. Though I prefer to see you on top of an elephant." I knew this reference to the time he led into battle an armored African circus elephant to fight French mercenaries in Virginia City would make him smile and sure enough, he was grinning.

"You look uncertain," he observed. "You must stop eating roasted sand larks from the Indians at Sun Mountain. Your skin is dark, but your stomach is very white."

"It's true that no one cooks a desert bird," I said, "better than you."

Impatient with our banter, Cutter, Snake's elder and a legendary warrior in Nevada, raised his rifle, taking aim at the one-wheeled Annihilators. "Circus clowns," he said gruffly. "But they fight like demons."

"Let me join in the fight," I said to Cutter, my life hanging on a precarious thread.

"No," Snake said. "There's already commotion in town. Take the children back there and protect your wife."

"Is—is she in trouble?"

"Your father is there with a hundred guns, drinking and intimidating. You were drawn here as a distraction. My brothers and I will wipe out these Texans."

"Give 'em hell, Snake."

Ezra climbed back onto my horse behind me, and the Paiute allowed us to pass and move toward the rocky ledge. Then we caught speed, the sound of our hoofbeats pounding the rugged landscape.

As we reached the safety of a ledge overlooking the ravine, I paused to glance back at Snake and his warriors. In an effort to change the terms of engagement, they'd maneuvered their horses onto a wide mesa below the path we'd been on, positioning themselves strategically among rocks and brush, bows and rifles at the ready.

———

I FELT LIKE HELL, but knew I'd feel worse leaving Snake to fight the Annihilators.

"Take the kids back to Virginia City," I said to Buzzard. "My buddy Snake doesn't know what he's in for. I can't let him die here on the mountain."

"You're in no condition to fight. Sounds like your wife needs you."

"Kid," Ezra pleaded, "come with us."

"Let me stay," Sarah said, still eager to tangle with the Texans. "Those fools don't scare me."

I shook my head. "Tell Chaparral and Jericho to avoid Tom Molyneaux," I said to the kids, "until I get there."

Buzzard scratched his head. "Molyneaux the bareknuckle boxer? Your father runs with a serious crowd."

"You have no idea. Sarah?" I dismounted, leaving my horse to Ezra and her, but I kept the canteen of water.

"Yes?"

"Any more bullets for that Derringer?"

She walked up to me and handed me the gun and two more bullets from her pocket. I loaded her pistol, knowing it wasn't much firepower.

"Stay close to Bad Jace. He's a little gruff, as you know, but he won't let anything happen to you."

"Got it." She jumped on my saddle in front of Ezra and was about to slap the reins.

"Wait!" I yelled.

"What?"

"You and Ezra—do not go anywhere near my father. Understand?"

Ezra and Sarah looked at each other and nodded in solemn confirmation.

"Go!" I said, watching them as their horses kicked up dust.

I turned back toward the battle about to rage on the side of the mountain, taking sips of water as I trudged up the incline. Soon I heard gunfire and screams as a dust storm began gathering, spinning debris into a funnel along the ridge above the mesa where I'd left Snake.

I nearly lost my hat in the wind as I hiked a sandstone ramp to get a view of the fight. The mesa, covered in desert shrubs and pinyons, spread out like a rumpled carpet. From behind a boulder, I peered down with the percussion cap in my right hand, the Derringer in my left.

The carnage was severe. Two of Snake's warriors had been shot dead already, blood still pouring into the dirt. The sight of this horror stirred the monster inside me, the beast straining against a leash of exhaustion and blows to the head and neck. I wasn't close enough for a shot and there wasn't an easy way to get down the cliff band, so I scrambled down a sun-savaged pinyon whose roots sprouted out of the ledge, providing a kind of rickety ladder to the mesa.

As I came around the ridge, I saw the Annihilator with the coffee-mill gun had lost his weapon, but he was straddling a supine Paiute, fingers on the warrior's throat, strangling him. Rage boiled my heart and I got within a few feet to pull the trigger of the percussion cap. It misfired, singeing my fingers as it leaped from my hand like a catfish.

When I raised the Derringer, the Annihilator had a moment to react, swinging behind him to tangle my arm and yank the gun away, sending it flying into the dirt.

He spun around to get behind me with the intent to roll me and slam me onto my back. I'd spent too much time brawling in pits for that to work, so I broke his grip, pushed his mitt down against my back pocket, and spun around to wallop him in the face.

He staggered backward, unaware the Paiute he'd been choking was on his feet now with a blade. The warrior raked the knife under the Annihilator's chest, a pitiless death strike, his kidney perforated and blood gushing everywhere. The mercenary fell to his knees, gurgle-whimpered, and keeled over to bleed out in the dust.

"Good riddance," I growled, the monster untethered and feral, the scent of blood all around.

I heard the sound of a bullwhip against the wind as it snagged the Paiute's neck and, with a sickening sound, broke it.

The Annihilator provided some slack to the whip, so the warrior's lifeless body could collapse to the ground with a thud. Then the mercenary cackled with satisfaction.

"Crimson Junior," he said, tonguing his lips like a reptile. "I'm going to enjoy lashing you."

15

WESLEY APPROACHED, MINCING WITH A theatrical aggression that repulsed me. With each step, he positioned himself to cut me off from a possible escape, nudging me closer to the edge of the mesa and a sheer drop off. The bullwhip was coiled at his side, leather straps promising a flesh rending. I didn't know how much more pain I could tolerate. My skull felt like it might split open from the recent and repeated beatings I'd sustained and I was exhausted to my core, but I couldn't leave Snake and Cutter here to die. At least one Annihilator had been dispatched and Wesley the whip-wielder was mine to kill. I had no idea about Styron the pikeman.

Having watched Wesley use his whip to snap the neck of a Paiute triggered my darkness. The wrath of the demon living inside me leaked from my pores, an oozing monster crafted by my father. I was the malevolent force he was all too proud to have sculpted, even if he wasn't strong or smart enough to contain it...or me. I was the chaos he yearned to wield like a weapon against the world, a tool of his design, an instrument for his rotten ambitions. But my father had allowed me to grow too lethal, too cunning. He pushed me too far, setting me loose in a landscape of slavery and war.

Here I was now, in a Nevada mining town, fighting mercenaries hired by Carson Crimson to extend his slavery and bloodshed out West. To be free of him, I had to kill his thugs and his army in Silver City. I had no intention of letting the Annihilators near everything I held dear. They'd die right here on the mountain, with my hands on their throats, my bullets in their brains, my knives in their hearts.

I slowly reached for the razor-sharp Bowie in my boot as Wesley's eyes locked onto me. There was no escape; it was a fight to death, and I was already at death's door. I had nowhere to go but forward and that meant an almost certain whip lashing. With a growl, I charged.

Anticipating my aggression, Wesley uncoiled his whip with a flick of his wrist. The knotted cords of the cat-o'-nine-tails lashed out with a crack. I ducked, the whip's tip slicing the air inches from my face. I closed the distance, forcing Wesley to adjust, but he was skilled at killing. The whip lashed again, grazing my shoulder and leaving a stinging welt.

The demon possessed me. Wesley saw it in my eyes and stopped laughing, his face going blank in a trance of murderous lust. He raised the lash again to tear me to gory ribbons.

With each crack of the whip, he sought to wear me down slowly. But I was a seasoned fighter, weaving with an agility learned from countless scrapes.

The moment I was waiting for finally presented itself. Wesley lost his balance for a twitch in time, and with a burst of speed, I lunged, narrowly avoiding another strike. My knife came up in a vicious arc aimed at Wesley's throat. Twisting his body, he deflected my blade with the handle of his whip. I pivoted and slashed again, this time aiming for his legs, slicing him deeply.

He inhaled sharply and cursed. "When I'm done lashing you to bloody bits," he said, "I'm going to have my way with your pregnant wife, then lynch her from the roof of her opium den and watch her dangle."

I recognized his attempt to render me blind with rage, but it also revealed his mounting desperation. His next lashing caught my knife hand, twisting it in an effort to force me off balance. But he made the mistake of dragging me into a boulder, where he'd abrade me and bash my skull. Instead, I stretched the leather strap across the top of the rock and slashed it with my knife, the sudden loss of tension knocking him on his butt.

Desperate to find cover, he turned his back on me, scrambling. I flipped the knife in the air, caught it by the tip, and hurled the blade into his spine.

With an agonizing shriek, he fell forward on his face. Crawling in the dust and sobbing, he reached behind himself with an arm to yank out the knife. But he couldn't find the angle to wrench it free.

I walked up behind him and placed the sole of my boot against the handle, pressing down.

He squealed again, his body spasming in pain.

I turned him onto his side to face me.

"No, you bastard, you won't do anything to my wife —or anyone, ever again."

I picked up a heavy rock. "I'll see you in hell," I said, watching his eyes grow wider and more fearful as I brought it down once, crushing the front of his head.

I ripped out the blade and wiped it on his clothes. Then I ran back to the last of the fight.

Searching for Snake, I found him covered in dust, hooked by Styron's pike and being dragged to the edge of the steepest part of the mesa. Badly injured, Cutter was on his knees, struggling to keep his balance, his hand clutching the wound on his shoulder. He was staring at the ground like there might be something there worth picking up.

Grinning like a madman, Styron seemed ecstatic. He was about to drop Snake, legs hanging off the edge, three hundred feet into the rocky gorge below. I spotted the Derringer Wesley had ripped from my hand, picked it up, and lobbed it at my Paiute buddy.

"Snake!"

The gun arced in his direction.

It was a perfect throw. Snake snapped it out of the air and pointed it at the pikeman.

Styron's expression was as shocked as if he'd just seen magic. The Indian warrior squeezed off both rounds, the first tearing into his throat and the second smashing into his cheek. The last Annihilator died wheezing blood.

Snake retreated from the edge of the mesa, rubbing his shoulder where the pike had torn flesh.

"I don't owe you now," I said, leaning forward on my knees as the terrain started spinning.

"Owe me for what?" Snake's voice was low and shattered from the fight.

"Saving my life at Pyramid Lake."

Snake laughed. "You'll never settle that debt."

"What do you mean?"

"You were dead when I found you."

"Well, you brought me back to life." My legs gave out from under me and I fell to the ground.

"No. I summoned a demon in your place."

———

WE PILED rocks atop Snake's three warriors, marking their location, so Grover could drive up with his wagon at some point and prepare them for a proper Paiute funeral. If he still had a wagon. We bandaged Cutter's shoulder wound and the three of us saddled up the dead men's horses and headed down the mountain. I did my best not to fall into the scrub.

Snake didn't like the looks of me. "You need medicine, Tiny. You remind me of coyote scat."

"I need a bath, a steak, and rest. No time. I have to get back to my town and my family."

"You need croco-dragon serum."

"Ha. You mean Dr. Skorpion's proprietary blend of, what was it? Soothing herbs and healing Seneca oil."

"Extracted," Snake continued, talking in his white man voice, "from the rarest glands of the powerful croco-dragons in the mystical reaches of Bolivia."

"Animals that live for five hundred years!" I said, finishing Skorpion's famous sales pitch.

"Seriously, have you tried it?"

"I don't believe in Skorpion's hogwash elixir." The switchbacks were fierce on this part of the trail, and I made a clicking noise to keep my horse moving.

"It gives you strength."

"Snake, I can't tell if you're joking."

"We'll all have some. Cutter loves the feeling it affords."

"It's true," Cutter said, smiling weakly.

I gave Snake a skeptical look. "You travel with a canteen of croco-dragon serum?"

He laughed. "We'll stop here for a moment and buy a batch from the good doctor direct."

Tunnel-visioned, I didn't notice Dr. Skorpion's wagon set up in a camp of prospectors working a vein that crested against the last ridge of the mountain we were descending.

"I don't know if I'll keep the stuff down," I said, already nauseated.

"Relax, Tiny. We'll chase it with whiskey."

Up ahead, a dappled horse, coat flecked with the grime of a long journey, stood patiently as Dr. Skorpion entertained a ragtag collection of miners and soiled doves forming a semi-circle around the wagon. Skorpion wore a powder-blue tailcoat, his wagon draped with vibrant, tattered banners proclaiming "Miracle Elixir!" and "Cure-All Snake Oil!" A crumpled top hat perched atop his graying hair, Skorpion exuded an aura of confident flamboyance.

Snake and I dismounted and joined the audience, leaving Cutter in his saddle, head down and chin resting on his chest. With a flourish, the medicine man produced a small vial of his dubious elixir, its contents swirling in a rich, oily amber. He cleared his throat. "Step right up, folks! Witness the marvel of the ages, an elixir that cures your aches and promises to make the weak strong and the old young!"

Snake and I exchanged a glance as Skorpion, spying the recently arrived Confederates, poured two small doses of the elixir into tin cups, dropping a slice of lemon into each. With an exaggerated bow, he presented the cups to us.

"I assure you, gentlemen, this serum is a fountain of vitality. Go on. Have a taste."

Snake accepted his cup with a nod, his expression unreadable. I peered into the liquid warily before tipping it back.

The liquid was heavy, fiery, an odd blend of herbs and something vaguely metallic. It was the worst, most ferocious alcohol I'd ever tasted. My tongue was left hanging and I didn't dare draw it in for fear of bringing more of the tincture into my reeling mouth.

I looked at Snake, his gaze inscrutable. He nodded once, took a sip...and hissed like an impaled Gila in reaction.

The men gathered with us, for whatever reason, smiled at our response to this dangerous liquid. They clamored for Skorpion to sell them each a bottle, clutching dollar bills in one hand as he happily distributed his croco-dragon serum with the other.

"I remember it tasting better," Snake said, disappointed.

"It's terrific," I said, reaching for my wallet. "Dr. Skorpion, ten bottles, please!"

"I see now. You plan to give this tincture to your worst enemy."

"In a way. They won't be drinking it, though."

Snake stared into the bottom of his empty cup. "We often used whiskey the white men sold us to create bottle bombs to burn settlers' homes."

Skorpion walked over to us carrying a crate of serum. "You won't regret this, Kid."

"I'm sure I won't," I said. "We're going to need a gig to pull your tincture into town."

"There's one propped right behind my wagon. Take it. On the house."

"You're too generous, Skorpion."

He laughed. "I should take you and your Indian friend on the road with me. The way you respond to the strength serum is better than a full-page advertisement in the *Territorial Enterprise*."

A roughneck in the crowd, who didn't appreciate that I'd purchased Skorpion's last dozen serums, pushed his way toward us and confiscated a bottle from my crate.

"You can't claim all these serums for yourself, son," he said. "Some of us men work for a living and need this kind of rejuvenation."

"Dayton, there's no need to—" Skorpion interjected.

Dayton, clearly blasted from a long day of drinking, backhanded Skorpion. He popped the cork and took a swig, wiped his mouth, then stared nastily at Snake.

"Indian," he said, "I'm giving you five seconds to get moving. This here is our bonanza and you're not entitled to any of it."

When he went to take another swig, Snake took the Winchester off his shoulder and used the stock to smack the bottle from the man's hands. As the bottle flew in the air, Snake fired, the bottle exploding into a fireball that prompted everyone, save for Snake and me, to hit the dirt.

"You're right, Kid," Snake said. "This serum is golden."

16

Back in Virginia City, I saw anxious, gloomy faces. My arrival was greeted with a mixture of relief—after all, I was the town's de facto sheriff—and dread, given the inevitable violence. I didn't see my father anywhere, but the noise emanating from the Blood Nugget and the dozens of horses tethered to hitching posts suggested that he'd summoned a significant number of men to tonight's magic show at the opera house. Virginia City had held big events that drew people from neighboring towns before, but the atmosphere this time was sinister. Ralston had failed to warn me of the possibility of a soft invasion, and I figured I'd try to find out why.

If there ever was another meeting.

Clementine Dunn greeted me with a canteen of cold water. Her eyes were bright with affection and if I hadn't felt so terrible, I would've swept her up in my arms and kissed her.

"Poppy is in labor," she said, bringing a hand to my

cheek, while trying to temper her excitement. "Your baby is almost here."

"What?" I said. "It's a few weeks early! I swear to God, if Scullard lays a hand—"

"Hush. Chaparral's girlfriend Rosie is delivering. Come with me now."

She took me by my bloodied arm, leading me to Poppy's buggy. She hopped into the seat as I, however, struggled to step up.

"Let me help, Kid," Hank said, suddenly at my side.

"You're back from the Salt Lake City route," I said, leaning on his shoulder for a boost.

"Denver, actually. Had trouble on the way back."

"What kind of trouble?" Finally seated in the buggy, I flinched as Dunn wiped my dirty, sweaty brow with her handkerchief.

"Stage robbers. And they used an interesting weapon."

"I'll take a stab. Trebuchet?"

Hank nodded. "Your father hemmed us in, Kid. Bad Jace got us through it. But now, Crimson Senior is in Virginia City."

"Captain Connor is off fighting Indians, I imagine."

"An inapt time for that," Dunn chimed in. "Given Virginia City has been overrun."

"Anyhow, don't let me keep you," Hank said, starting to pat my leg before seeing I was fragile.

"I suspect," I said, "I'll need your expertise, Hank, if we survive tonight's extravaganza."

"I'm here for you, Kid. I'd ride with you straight through the gates of hell."

"That might be exactly where we're headed."

THE HOUSE I shared with Poppy and the kids had never looked so welcoming and cozy. An earthy scent of fresh herbs and boiling water mingled in the air, providing a sense of calm. Clementine made me wash up in a tub of sudsy hot water that had been prepared for me. I kept nodding off as she scrubbed me from crown to toes, paying special attention to removing the grit from under my nails.

"You can't hold your baby if you're covered in blood," she said, smiling.

She made me eat a few bites of a steak she'd broiled for me. She brought me denim jeans, shirt, and moccasins, and together we went into the bedroom. The large, sturdy frame upon which Poppy and I had conceived our child was now draped in white linens, candles flickering on the dresser and armoire. The stove in the corner crackled gently, its warmth contributing to a soothing ambience. Amid this tranquil setting, Rosie, a beacon of calm, played the role of Mormon midwife, tending to my lovely Poppy.

Poppy lay on the bed, face flushed, but radiant with the joy and anticipation of this moment. Knowing how unsteady I was on my feet, Clementine led me to my wife's side. I clasped Poppy's hand. The room buzzed with quiet, heartfelt encouragement as Poppy's friends— Verbena, the schoolteacher Lydia Sweet, Emma from House of Hammers, and Winnie the pasty-maker—gathered close, their presence a testament to the tight-knit distaff side of Virginia City, a mining town saturated in gunpowder and greed.

With measured, gentle, and reassuring movements, Rosie kept her voice serene, offering words of encouragement to Poppy, guiding her through each contraction.

Verbena assisted by dabbing Poppy's brow with a cool, damp cloth, her touch tender and comforting.

Emma, seated in a nearby chair, held a worn Bible, lips moving in silent prayer as she watched over my wife.

Moments ticked by; anticipation grew. Poppy's breath quickened, yet her expression remained determined and cheerful. With encouragement from Rosie and a surge of effort from Poppy, the first cries of our newborn soon filled the room. Hearing the sound was a shot of pure, triumphant energy that stirred everyone's emotions.

Rosie was the first to carefully cradle the squirming bundle, her face breaking into a tearful smile before handing my child to Poppy. "You have a son, darling," she said.

Wrapped in a hand-sewn blanket, the baby was perfect and pink, eyes blinking open to take in the world for the first time. Outside, explosions continued, only they didn't vex me in this moment.

Poppy held our baby close. I sensed her heart swelling with love, just like mine. I leaned in to inspect the child.

"A son!" I said, unable to help myself. "I knew it. Thank God."

I kissed Poppy on the lips once, twice, thrice.

"I always wanted a boy," Poppy said, exhausted yet beaming.

Suddenly, the women in the room erupted into a chorus of cheers and heartfelt congratulations. They gathered round, eager to share in the messy miracle of new life.

I noticed that Rosie, her work done, took a step back to wash her hands in the basin. She surveyed the scene with satisfaction, absorbing the laughter, the cooing, the sound of happiness.

"Thank you, Rosie," I said, my voice cracking slightly.

"Congratulations, Kid. Don't let him grow up to be a gun."

"Not this one. My son Glade will be a lawyer."

"Glade?"

"Short for 'Everglade.'"

"That," Verbena said, "is a terrible name."

"Everglade Gawain Crimson."

"It's getting worse. Someone stop him, please." Verbena looked at the other women.

"Gawain?" Emma said. "What the heck?"

"King Arthur's nephew and one of the Knights of the Roundtable."

"Jesus," Verbena. "Oops, sorry, Rosie and Emma. Look, I think Poppy gets a say on the name."

"I don't care what we call him," my wife blubbered. "He's just so beautiful!"

———

I WANTED to stay with Poppy and Glade all night, but there was the issue of the magic show. I kissed my wife on her sleeping forehead, kissed my newborn son's dark, manic mane, and donned a fresh suit that Poppy had laundered for me, including my bright red cravat. I pulled on my long black riding boots, then took down from the attic my backup Colt Army Model 1860 single-action revolver and cleaned it.

Clementine was still in the house and observed me preparing for violence. She couldn't square what she was witnessing with the earlier scene of my son's arrival. "You can't be serious," she said, crossing her arms.

"About what?"

"About cleaning a weapon with your son in the next room."

"Why do you say that?"

"Because your baby was created out of love. And here you are loading a widow maker."

"My gun made it possible for my son to arrive. My gun is here so my son will never need to pick one up himself. My gun is here to eliminate my bloodthirsty father."

"I can't believe I washed blood off *you*, so you can put more back on."

"Clementine, nothing has changed just because my son is here."

"Everything has changed, Kid."

"For me and Poppy, sure, but Virginia City remains in danger. You know that. The world spins on. It doesn't stop just because my wife and I enjoyed a tender moment."

"You can't continue, Kid. What I know is, if you keep living with the gun, you'll die by it."

"You've no idea how many damn times I've died, Clementine—"

"You promised to become a father!"

"Why are you yelling at me? We're not even married," I said, trying to bring levity.

This shut her up for a moment. Then she said, "I—I guess I feel a sense of responsibility."

"Why?"

"I ushered you into the world of dime novels, and… and I want to pen a happy ending for you."

"I'm not a character you can control."

"I—I realize that."

She moved closer to me, placing her hand on my chest. It didn't feel lustful. It felt…well, it felt like something else entirely.

I cleared my throat. "I'm going to save Virginia City

one final time. And then I'm moving my family to Sonoma County to a grapefruit farm. And we're going to have the happy ending that you want for me in California, with more babies, and Ezra and Sarah and Glade and their brothers and sisters growing strong and tall in the orchards, in the sun, and away from the stench of gunpowder and strychnine."

"I'd love that for you, Kid." She looked down at the floor, ashamed of something, but couldn't figure what.

"Come with us," I offered. "New York is a shithole full of draft riots and grinding poverty."

"Yes, it's true, but writing books and magazine articles is all I know."

It was my turn to draw close. I touched her perfectly dimpled chin, lifting her face to look up at me. I removed her glasses and placed them on the table. Her eyes were gorgeous, intoxicating. Her long blonde hair was out of a dream.

"Why did you show up in Virginia City, Clementine?"

"I told you. I came here to learn more about you, so I can write more Kid Crimson books."

"Are you in love with me?"

She rolled her eyes, scoffed. "Well, not in the way you mean."

"What does that—"

She took a step backward and said, "Brace yourself. This will come as something of a shock."

My patience was wearing thin. "Out with it."

"All right. Here it is. I believe we have the same father."

I felt my legs buckle for a moment, reaching for the table to keep from toppling over. "You—you're Carson's daughter? From his other family?"

"Yes. So you're aware that he spent time in New York

—when he attended West Point. My mother was the heiress to the Spear fortune. She lived in Peekskill near the Academy."

"Were they married?"

"No."

I wasn't surprised. My father would never tie himself down legally. But the way Clementine dropped her head, as if in shame, I suspected there might have been some coercion involved with her conception. I tried to process everything I was hearing and experiencing—a newborn son and a half sister, all in the same half-hour. But I was coming up so short, I could barely string together a coherent thought. "I always had the strongest feeling that...that...you...existed. I just didn't expect to... ever..."

A crowd of voices boomed from B Street, in front of my home, climbing the hill to the opera house. Thurston Larue's magic show was about to start.

"We have a lot to discuss," I said, "at a later date. Right now I need to stop my father."

"Let me accompany you to the opera house."

"I'd welcome it. You might need to prop me up. I should mention to you the bath was delightful, and the steak delicious."

"Good," she said. "Lean on me, Kid. I'll guide you to the buggy."

———

THE TOWN WAS abuzz with excitement as the crowd— hundreds of miners and their families, curious travelers, and bankers from California—made their way to the grandest building on A Street: the opera house. This evening, the venue was set to showcase an entertainer unlike any other in the West: a magician renowned for his ability to escape any trap.

Though modest compared to city theaters, the opera house exuded a rustic elegance, its wooden façade decorated with faded posters illuminated by lanterns flickering invitingly against the encroaching darkness. Clementine and I stepped inside to find the hall alive with the murmurings of people eager to witness a spectacle rife with mystery and suspense.

The interior was opulent, yet cozy. Red-velvet curtains framed the stage, set with a backdrop of draped fabric and a large wooden wardrobe. Gas lamps cast a glamorous glow over the audience. The scent of pine and tobacco mingled in the air as people took their seats, their chatter reaching a crescendo as the performance time approached.

Clementine and I sat in the second to last row of the auditorium. I'd have preferred the very last row; I wanted my back to a wall and the fastest escape route. But all those seats were full. The best I could do was to grab the aisle seat.

"My father isn't here," I said. "It's mostly miners from town and, from the looks of it, Silver City."

Clementine frowned. "I don't see him either. Maybe he's out to rattle our nerves?"

"Bad Jace is here, sitting near the front."

"Your bartender friend Jericho just walked in. Seems like he's watching the doors."

"My friends are solid."

Larue strutted out onto the stage, dressed in a sharply cut suit and top hat the color of Alaska salmon, and stood at the center with poise, commanding the room. Dominick Myles, the opera house owner, introduced the magician with dramatic flair before settling in the front row. Larue was met with enthusiastic applause, and he took a moment to bow, acknowledging the crowd with a smile. Then he cued Chaparral, piano player at the Blood Nugget, to provide musical accompaniment in the orchestra pit, so he could launch his act with help of a young female assistant.

Finally, Larue spoke to the audience, his words painting a picture of wonder.

"Tonight, my friends, you'll encounter the end of the material realm and the start of the spirit dimension when I bring to you...the Portals of Disappearance!"

He explained his trick with flair, emphasizing the wardrobe's solid structure—he rapped it with knuckles—and the impossibility of its contents vanishing. Larue's voice, rich and engaging, resonated through the theater as he built up the suspense.

"From the audience, I require a volunteer! Please, stand up if you'd like to participate!"

No one accepted the invitation. The crowd started to twitter, while Larue stood there amused. Finally, a young woman stood and Larue immediately pointed, calling out, "You! The beautiful lady in the middle. Let her through! Let her through!"

Dressed in a modest gown, she approached the stage and was helped by Larue. She appeared excited and apprehensive. With the magician's reassuring words, she stepped into the wardrobe, her silhouette briefly visible through the open doors before they closed behind her.

We all leaned forward, our collective breath held as the magician began his incantations, his hands moving weirdly as he performed a series of dramatic gestures. The room seemed to throb with anticipation as Larue opened the wardrobe doors. To our astonishment, the wardrobe was empty, bare as a Scotchman's knee. Gasps rippled through the crowd, followed by a wave of applause and incredulous laughter.

Then Larue, with a bow, stepped aside to reveal the young woman emerging from behind the curtains on stage's opposite side. The miner's wife was met with cheers, her smile wide with relief and delight.

The magician's skillful execution of the trick left us spellbound, skepticism replaced by wonder.

But then the show went in a direction I didn't anticipate, but should have.

"For this next demonstration, I require not one, but two volunteers! Stand if you're willing to enter another dimension!"

This time, a number of couples stood, raising and waving their hands. Children from all over the room were jumping and down, yelling, "Pick us! Pick us!" Larue scanned the crowd, then looked down at two kids standing in the front row, pointed, and said, "You two!"

Ezra and Sarah.

I groaned and grabbed Clementine's hand. "I have a bad feeling about this."

"Me too."

"I need to stop the show."

I started to stand up in the dark when from behind, a rough hand grabbed my jaw and I felt the pinch of a knife pressed to my neck.

"You're just going to sit here and watch," a voice growled in my ear. I recognized it. It belonged to the boxer, Tom Molyneaux. Beside me, another pair of hands gripped Clementine, a blade against her cheek.

With practiced ease, Larue guided my kids, waving at the audience, into a new box, a chest lined with plush velvet and surprisingly spacious. Then the magician closed the lid, locking it with a resounding click, and turned to face us. His hands moved in an elaborate sequence as he began his incantation, his voice rising in a crescendo.

I strained against Molyneaux's grip, but he tightened it and pressed the blade deeper into my neck.

The room was thick with chatter and anticipation, everyone waiting to see the chest opened to reveal the empty space where the two young volunteers had been. And sure enough, when Larue opened the chest, it was empty. Applause erupted, stronger than for the young woman, and Larue basked in the glory as his outstretched arm signaled for the kids to emerge from the left wing.

However, as the moments ticked by, an uneasy murmur began to ripple through the crowd.

Larue's expression of concentration shifted to concern. His demeanor faltered. The audience's murmurs grew louder, confusion and apprehension clouding the once-cheerful atmosphere.

Ezra and Sarah failed to reappear. As the seconds ticked by, a gasp of horror and surprise swept through the opera house. Larue, his face pale with beads of sweat forming on his brow, ran off stage to the left, then ran across the stage to the right, then walked slowly, his head down, staring at the floor, and turned his back on the audience.

He'd lost them both.

I'd lost them too.

17

Held at knifepoint by Tom Molyneaux and two other men whose faces I couldn't see in the theater lighting, one took my pistol and both were pointing guns at us. Clementine and I were shoved through a side door and into the alley, where a six-horse stagecoach was waiting for us. Sitting in the driver's seat was Hank Monk, looking grim. One of my father's men had a gun on him, and I noticed this was the carriage on which Hank and I had encountered the Annihilators in Devil's Gate en route to Silver City. I was glad to see both Hank and the coach.

Knife against my throat, I felt my arms being bound, a strip of cloth roughly pressed against my mouth. A hemp sack thrown over my head, I was blind, and I assumed they did the same to my half sister.

"Enjoy your short trip to oblivion," Molyneaux said, shoving me inside. "Sorry I can't join you."

He laughed in the night and, from what it sounded like, got on a horse and rode off.

I made a note to spend a few minutes punching the mirth out of Molyneux when I saw him next time.

I heard Clementine start to scream as they dragged her toward the carriage. There was the sound of an open-handed slap, followed by a whimper. Soon, her body collided with mine. We struggled and failed to get upright and find our balance on the carriage floor.

A stage whip cracked, the stage rumbling, moving up A Street in the direction of the mines, the wheels creaking and clattering over a debris-littered, muck-pocked road.

I had no doubt we'd be dropped down an abandoned shaft to our deaths, Hank along with us. I didn't wish to die this way, having just met my sibling for the first time and watched my adopted kids vanish during a magic act conducted by a complicit, or ignorant illusionist. A hail of bullets had to provide the curtain. It was all I'd accept.

I tried to speak, but the gag muted my words. As I rolled to my side and brought my knees to my chest, I sensed Clementine's bound hands searching for leverage to help her get off the floor. I pushed the side of my boot toward her, hoping her fingertips detected the handle of my Bowie.

She found it. I could feel her slide the blade from my boot. She pretzeled herself in an effort to cut her bonds. "Hold still, Kid."

Within seconds, the knife was slicing back and forth against rope and my arms were free. I removed my gag, slipped off the hood, and when the stage hit a pothole slammed my head against the carriage door.

Clementine embraced me. "Where are they taking us?"

"To a mountain mineshaft, where they plan to drop us like a sounding rock."

"They've got Hank at gunpoint."

"Well, I have them at gunpoint," I said, reaching into the hidden nook behind the passenger seats. I'd stashed the pepperbox pistol there days ago for just this kind of emergency.

"My ingenious baby brother."

"You have no idea," I said, winking at her. I opened the passenger door and swung out, holding on to the door so I could point the pepperbox at Carson's man sitting in the perch.

The angle was all wrong, however. To avoid the risk of my bullet going through the gunman and striking Hank, I tapped the villain on the shoulder. He turned in surprise and as he brought his pistol around, I yanked his arm, pulling him out of his seat so that he slammed into the dust below, the back end of the slow-moving stage smashing his head open, nearly shattering the wheel.

Hank pulled on the reins, eliciting a surge of anger as I climbed into the shotgun seat. "We're heading back to town!"

Realizing I was incensed, Hank rein-slapped the team of horses, making a sharp turn at the edge of town that nearly sent me flying. "Kid, they used a gun on me. I didn't want to—"

"I'm not mad, Hank. I need Larue to return Ezra and Sarah to me. And I need to...have a word with Molyneux."

"The young'uns are missing?"

"The magician made them...disappear."

Clementine climbed into the driver's seat between Hank and me. "They're not really gone. It's an illusion."

"Larue didn't have control. Something went wrong."

Whether by accident or intent, Hank ran his horses

over the corpse of my father's henchman. Jostled from the impact, Clementine threw her arms around me for balance.

"Oops," Hank said, winking at her.

"We need," Clementine said, "to find Larue."

I held her close. "That won't be hard. Bad Jace and Chaparral and Jericho have him tied up in the Blood Nugget storeroom."

Clementine looked up at me. "How do you know that?"

"Worked with them for years. We have what you might call a telepathic bond."

"Especially Kid and Bad Jace," Hank explained. "They're like two different sides of the same coin. Bad Jace is messy and monstrous. Kid is dapper and deadly. They make a good duo, but I prefer doing jobs with Kid. Bad Jace is noisy and too often shoots coyotes along the trail."

"Why does he do that?" she asked.

I stepped in to clarify as the Blood Nugget came into view. "His girlfriend, Lydia Sweet, the schoolteacher, explained it to me. Bad Jace was bitten by starving coyotes when his parents abandoned him as a child a few miles from an Indian tribe in Missouri. The Kickapoo rescued him in time, but he still lost a pinky finger."

"He grew up among Indians?"

"Yes, but he didn't appreciate the experience."

"Here you go, Kid," Hank said, pulling up in front of Verbena's bar. "Mind if I join you?"

"Not at all." I stepped off the stage. "We have a lot to discuss with the Shadow Man."

"I hope he makes it easy on himself."

"If there's one thing I can guarantee you, it's that Larue spills everything."

I helped Clementine from the driver's seat as she continued writing in her notepad. "Why do you say that?"

"Magicians are deceivers. And a deceiver is a man who can't be strong in the face of pain."

"Wow, I used to think magicians were attractive."

"Clementine, um…you never…" I held open one of the batwings of the Blood Nugget.

She turned red, punched my arm, and walked into the saloon. "With Thurston Larue? Absolutely disgusting, Kid. Go wash your mouth out with mercury."

"Now who's being gross!"

"Excuse me for noticing," Hank said, "but you seem to share a sibling affection for each other. It's not a fondness that Kid usually displays for the opposite sex."

I didn't know what to say to this, so I stayed quiet.

———

AS I'D PREDICTED, Thurston Larue was tied to a chair in the dimly lit storeroom of the Blood Nugget. Jericho, head bandaged and sleeves rolled up and looking impatient, held a big, waxy, burning candle near the magic man's face, making him sweat profusely. His jacket and top hat were gone, his hair disheveled and greasy, and there was a cut under his eye where Bad Jace had struck him.

Jericho saw me and apologized. "They clocked me from behind. Sorry I let you down, Kid."

I indicated I wasn't upset with him. "The magic trick had us off balance."

Chaparral stepped forward to greet me. "We figured you'd been dragged to Silver City."

"We almost were. But Clementine unshackled us and we got free."

"Good to hear you're safe now, ma'am," Chaparral said, doffing his derby. "You too, Hank."

"Where's he hiding Ezra and Sarah?" Hank got right down to the business at hand.

"The trick has always worked!" Larue said, fear elevating his voice into a higher register. "The kids were supposed to run onto the stage—the boy from one side and the girl from the other. Someone had to've grabbed them. I have no idea where they are."

Bad Jace didn't smoke, but he had a cigarette case, which he opened for me. I took a cigarette and waited for him to light it. Bad Jace struck a match against a barrel of rice and I used it to ignite the tobacco. I didn't smoke either.

"Who switched the chest?" I said to Larue.

When he looked at me, then at Clementine, I could see that he realized he'd seen us before and was trying to place us. Then he said, "You're the one with the spirit coffin. You must know how the trick works. Did you see anything?"

I was trying to decide if Larue was creating another illusion or was truly in the dark about it all. I glanced at Clementine and she shrugged; she couldn't be sure either.

"How did you happen to pick those two children?" she asked him.

"They were right there in the front row, jumping up and down. How could I miss them?"

"Where do you think they are now?"

Hands still lashed behind him, Larue shrugged. "My only guess is backstage in the opera house..."

Chaparral looked at me, shaking his head, indicating he'd searched backstage.

Bad Jace gave me a subtle nod, so I took the cigarette and brought the lit end close to Larue's eye. "You're going to start talking for real now."

"I'm—I'm telling you everything. It's all true, I swear."

"When your stagecoach was robbed in Devil's Gate, you went with Carson's men," Clementine said. "Why?"

"They—they gave me a choice. Go with them to Silver City or…" He trailed off.

"Or they'd kill you in a slow and creative fashion."

Larue hung his head and nodded.

"What happened in Silver City?" I asked.

"I was taken to the head man there, Carson Crimson. You've heard of him, I presume?"

"By reputation," from Clementine.

"A most interesting man in person. He has the eyes and manner of a vicious killer, but he has refined taste. He's an aesthete in many ways. And I should know. I've performed, as you know, for the most important men in the country. President Lincoln is an admirer—"

"Shut up about the Rail-splitter," Bad Jace growled.

"We know plenty about Lincoln," I said, bringing the cigarette closer. "We do his dirty work, which includes dropping you down an abandoned mine shaft."

Clementine made a noise of disgust. "I think he's in on it."

"In on what?!" Larue nearly screeched, sweat dripping from his face.

"The disappearance of those two children," I said.

"The conspiracy to destroy the mines in Virginia City," Clementine added.

"I—I don't know anything about a conspiracy."

I'd had enough of the blubbering warlock. I didn't know if he was an active participant in my father's strategy, but there was one way to find out.

"That settles it," I said. "You're coming with us."

"Where are you going?"

"Silver City."

"No no. I can't go back there."

"Why not?"

"Because…it's not the most sophisticated town for a magician."

"You need your magic chest. Besides, if you don't go," I said, my cigarette close enough to singe his eyelashes, "you're falling down a forgotten mineshaft. Without the use of your eyes."

Larue blinked rapidly and coughed once, as if he could already taste the poisoned air of a deep hole inside the Comstock. "Fine. I'll travel with you to Silver City."

I pulled back the cigarette and took a puff, but I didn't smoke so I passed it to Clementine.

"And you'll return the children," she said, exhaling a plume.

"As soon as I find them, if I ever do, I'll hand them right over to you."

"Wait," Chaparral said. "What if he gets killed before we find the chest?"

Bad Jace grunted. "He should give us the combination now."

"It's a mechanism, actually," Larue said.

"Whatever it is," I said, "you'll open it when the time comes."

"Yes, I'll do exactly that." Larue's eyes were bloodshot. "Can someone please untie me now?"

Bad Jace walked over, violently yanked the rope binding the magician's hands, and kicked the chair over, causing Larue to tip over and crash to the floor with a whimper.

I took Hank to the side and told him about the serums I'd brought with me from Dr. Skorpion's medicine wagon. "I need them loaded on a separate cart."

"Strength serum, huh? Figure you'll need it to beat that madman father of yours in Silver City?"

"I'll need it to cause a distraction in Silver City."

"I suspect," Hank said, "we'll have to make it past the trebuchet firing flaming projectiles at us as we navigate Devil's Gate."

"Yes," I said. "We need to upgrade your stagecoach into a war wagon."

"I've done some really dangerous routes crawling with bandits and Indians, bullets flying everywhere. But I've never dodged fireballs in an effort to invade a mining town."

"Clementine Dunn will chronicle it all for posterity. You'll be famous in dime novels," I told him.

"Fame is a vapor," my friend Sam Clemens said, stepping into the storeroom with dashing bravado, "popularity an accident; the only earthly certainty is oblivion."

"Sam!" Clementine said, rushing to greet him.

"Miss Dunn," he said, welcoming her with a hug.

"Are you ready, Sam," I said, "for your earthly certainty? We have a couple of kids to save."

"I can't think of a better way to spend a weekend. Actually, I can imagine many superior choices, but there's something about spending time with Kid Crimson that can't be topped."

"What is it, you think?"

"If I had to wager, I'd say it's your ability to generate never before seen havoc."

"I have new tricks that'll make Larue green with envy."

"Of that," Sam said, "I have no doubt."

18

Outside, a mob of dusty, deranged men—at least a hundred of my father's Silver City minions—greeted us as we exited the Blood Nugget. They carried mining tools, shovels, bottles, and knives.

The one in charge stepped forward, his face burned, I assumed, from hot oil thrown on him by Indians or someone he'd attempted to rob on the trails. He spoke low and crackling, as if his vocal cords had been injured. "You're not going anywhere, Kid. It'll all be over soon."

"If you try to stop us," I said, shielding Clementine, "the only thing that'll be over is your life."

"Silver City residents are tired of playing second fiddle to you Virginia City high-falutin' stuck-ups," he said. "We're taking over this town and running it our way."

"My father will never let you run anything. He'll have you all in chains, just like the slaves on his plantation."

I felt the tension rising in my buddies—Bad Jace, Chaparral, Jericho, and Sam Clemens. There weren't many of us, but we were capable of killing a few dozen of these lunatics before we fell. The men gathered before us knew this, which is why they hadn't immediately over-run us.

"A plantation like the one you grew up on?" Tom Molyneaux pushed through the crowd to square off with me. He was shirtless and sweaty, seemingly ready for a fistfight—in a saloon, outdoor boxing ring, or anywhere he found an opponent. "The pretty boy with the silver spoon thinks he knows slavery."

I glared at him while rolling up my sleeves. I wasn't in any condition for a bareknuckle brawl, but if I had to duke it out with him, providing time for Hank to show up with Skorpion serum, I would.

"Our experiences were different, Molyneaux," I said. "Mine was worse."

"Oh, so the white boy thinks his life of privilege was more painful than my life?" he said, addressing the crowd at this point. "I'm going to beat the stupid right out of this sumbitch."

"You're welcome to try," I growled. "But it won't go like you imagine it will."

Clementine grabbed my shirt. "Kid, your head can't handle this."

Bad Jace stiff-armed me, staring at Molyneaux with contempt. "Sit down, Crimson. I'll handle this mouthy clown."

The crowd started yelling at Jace to step aside, eager to see their boxing champion pummel me into mush. One of them picked up a piece of plywood, dragging it along the dirt to draw up the boundaries of a boxing ring. Another crazed spectator extended his arms, palms up, fluttering his fingers and wagging his tongue to indicate I should come forward and fight.

Realizing it was better to let me go ahead with it

given the mob's intensity, Chaparral and Jericho conferred with Bad Jace, who backed away from the crowd.

Soon, Molyneaux and I were in each other's faces, unblinking, fists clenched, and ready to throttle each other. Jericho, who'd refereed boxing matches before, was familiar to the Silver City men. They deferred to his experience, allowing him to step up and call the fight. He ordered us to stand in opposite corners of the crudely measured and marked ring.

As the men started placing bets on a ten-rounder, I grabbed my sister's arm to give her an important command. "When Hank arrives and tosses a bottle in the air," I said, keeping my voice low and laying my coat, gun belt, and hat on an old stump, "shoot it."

"I—I'm not a good shot," she said, using a handkerchief to wipe sweat from her face.

I smiled at her, then steeled myself for a clash with the champion boxer.

"No biting, no throwing sand in the eyes, no kicking the testicles!" Jericho said. "Let's fight!"

I remembered Molyneaux from our first fight, but now he looked huge, with chiseled shoulders and arms like knotted oaks. He stood a couple of inches taller than me, every ounce of his two-hundred-plus-pound body exuding lethal energy. Bulky but not oafish, he moved panther-like. Under dense eyebrows, his eyes sparkled with intelligent fierceness. He was quick, aggressive, and too tough to worry about a few punches slipping through his defense. The rarest of pugilists, he was a smart heavyweight with a death punch.

That was how I planned to take him down.

Someone gonged a tethered string of horseshoes with a shovel. Round one was underway.

I came very close to losing by a knockout in the first exchange. Charging in like a rabid animal, he landed first —a left-handed uppercut to my jaw, then a blasting right that dropped me to one knee. The right hit a little too high along the top of my skull, else I'd have fallen into a deep sleep.

I bounced up without a count and popped him with two consecutive jabs, dazing and enraging him. Furious, roaring like a wounded bull, he staggered me again with a crashing left to my collarbone. Chastened from my jabs, he remained in the center of the ring rather than press the attack.

"Kid, don't forget!" Sam Clemens called out to me. "It's not the size of the dog in the fight; it's the size of the fight in the dog!"

I ducked Molyneaux's next swing and countered with straight punch under his heart, which sent him reeling. He clinched up with me, and we danced clumsily for what felt like the rest of the first round, exchanging jabs. Soon I was gushing from the nose.

When I returned to my corner, Bad Jace gave no encouragement. "Let me throw in the towel if he gets over you. There's Poppy to think about, and Glade. I've been through too much with you to see your head get punched off."

His hands grasped mine, the grip of his iron fingers communicating his affection.

"Nothing doing. I've fought for my father since childhood. I'll go out the way I came in. There was never any other path. Tell Poppy I love her."

We embraced, and for a moment I didn't think he'd let go. I suspected he didn't want to. How could I tell him I was bent on my own demise? How could I tell him of my despair, my profound shame? My hideous father had arrived and successfully kidnapped half my family, and I'd failed to protect them. I was still that nine-year-old boy in the fighting pit of red clay Georgia, haunted by the phantom pain of all my mistakes.

Poppy would eventually choose one of her many suitors and Glade would have a real father. Without Ezra and Sarah, life meant nothing to me. So why not get it over with, finally? Why not lay down my life here for the pleasure of fools and alkies? It was all hopeless anyway. Or maybe there was still a chance I might excise the agony of my father from my memory forever? Given enough love, anything was possible. Poppy loved me and saved me from death many times.

Love might save me again.

Someone banged a piece of sheet metal with a miner's wrench, announcing the second round.

When Molyneaux erupted from his corner, a sense of horror overwhelmed me. Here was a fighter, I suddenly recalled, who'd knocked chained bears off their feet with his fist, and the fear of standing up and running full into such punches momentarily cowed me.

My head and body had been battered, probably beyond repair, in too many ways to recount, including my last fight against this hulk. Molyneaux had absorbed no damage then, obviously. He seemed fresher, healthier, more dangerous than ever.

Still, I set my jaw and prepared to fight on, bringing up my mitts and covering up as the punches rained down on me.

A hush fell over the crowd—a breathless silence as Hank Monk's horses suddenly interrupted the fight. Hank managed to get his coach between me and my friends, including Jericho, on one side and Molyneaux and the Silver City mob on the other.

"Better be handing out free whiskey, driver!" someone called out. "Otherwise, you just busted up a fight with big money on it for no good reason!"

"I do, in fact, have something you can all suck down!" Hank said, smiling.

With a wink to me and a hoot, he lobbed a bottle of Skorpion's strength serum high into the air.

Clementine raised the Winchester, took aim as the serum reached its apogee, and squeezed off a round.

She missed completely, the bottle landing with a clank at the boots of Molineaux.

"Kid," he said, chuckling as he stooped to pick up the container of amber liquid, his knuckles covered in my blood. "Your girlfriend can't shoot. After I'm done beating you senseless, I'll take her with me to Silver City and show her a few tricks."

He raised the bottle. When he brought it to his lips, Clementine fired again.

This time she hit the bull's eye.

Apart from the gunfire, the noise was minimal, but the sudden rush of heat and light was God-fearing. A blanket of fire covered the men at the edge of the crowd, burning them severely. Molyneaux, shrieking and completely enveloped in flames, raced like a nightmare toward a horse trough, flesh sizzling and smoking as he made contact with the water.

I didn't let the opportunity go to waste.

I climbed onto the luggage rack of Hank's stage, overlooking the Silver City mob, dozens of them on the ground screaming in agony as they tried to snuff the flames, dozens more peeling away in fright at having witnessed an orange globe of fire appear and scorch their buddies.

"There's more where that came from!" I yelled, my

fist in the air, sending a signal to Verbena to detonate the gunpowder barrels filled with nails and scrap metal that I'd asked Chaparral to stash on the other side of D Street, next to a yard of rusting mine equipment.

The explosion was thunderous, sharp metal bits slicing through the flesh of men caught running from the opera house fireball. They made terrible noises, clutching their wounds, some shredded in the eyes and throats, others gouged in the legs and, unable to run, hopping one-legged for cover behind parked wagons, thinking they'd been struck by cannon fire.

At that point, Uncle John John set loose Sarah's lion Uru, a four-hundred-pound jungle cat with a penchant for terrorizing people he didn't know too well. The beast scampered after and stalked anyone trying to escape, knocking them down and roaring his horrendous breath and gross spittle in their faces until they curled up into a ball. A few men tried to fight back against Uru using mining picks, which incited Bad Jace to gun them down with the Sharps rifle I'd let him borrow. Then Hannibal the elephant showed up, flipping over a freight wagon with its tusks and raising its trunk to trumpet a victory blast.

It was a rout.

With no one to lead them, the men still standing and mobile folded like a weak poker hand, getting back on their horses, returning to their buggies and buckboards, and heading in the direction of Silver City, tails between their singed, shrapnel-nicked legs.

"You're sending them back to Silver City?" Clementine said. "How's that going to help us?"

"They've had the fight knocked out of them. Cover your ears for a second." Bad Jace reloaded the Sharps and picked off a guy attempting to draw a rifle bead on Uru.

"These men are done riding Carson Crimson's power trip," he went on.

I slipped back into my coat, donned my cravat and hat, and walked over to where Molineaux had left his jacket to retrieve my Colt from his pocket. I didn't see the boxing champion anywhere and figured he was either dead or nursing his burns en route to Silver City.

I felt no satisfaction in any of it. I was bent, battered, and broken and there was a giant hole in the middle of me that only Ezra and Sarah could fill.

"Kid!"

When I looked up and turned in the direction of my name being called, I saw Chaparral approaching, shoving Thurston Larue, the magician, toward me, hands tied behind him.

He smiled, impressed with the carnage. "That was quite a trick you pulled off, Kid. You're a chaos magician."

"So you finally figured out who I am."

"Wasn't much of a challenge, with everyone yelling your name and referring to Carson Crimson as your father."

"Throw him in the coach," I said to Chaparral. "Clementine, you're riding with Hank and me."

"I've only been with you a few days," she said, examining the rifle in her hands, "and I've already swapped my pen for a gun."

"Kid has that effect on writers," my reporter friend Sam said, spinning the chamber on his pistol.

19

As Hank and Bad Jace prepared the stagecoaches for an assault on Silver City. I took the opportunity to see Rosie, the Mormon seer-stone gazer, in the kitchen of the apartment she shared with Chaparral. She expected my visit, given that I was now locked in epic combat with the man who'd somehow, in spiritual form, appeared to her and related warnings to me about earlier attacks on our mining town by outside forces.

"I need to know," I said to Rosie, "what my father is up to in Silver City."

We sat across from each other at a small table and held hands, the high desert sunshine streaming through a gap in the curtains she'd closed. A woven stick of sage burned in a ceramic bowl in an attempt, Rosie insisted, to mute any hostile energies being hurled in our direction.

"Your father has spoken to me directly twice," Rosie said. "Whether he speaks the truth or not, well..."

"Why does he talk to *you* of all people?"

"It's not intentional or conscious," she said. "Your father's messages are perhaps slumbering manifestations, his insensate mind reaching out to touch another phantasm in the ether."

"The ether of, what, dreams?"

She nodded. "Something like that."

"Rosie," I said, "I don't believe in all this esoteric foolery. But if you can help me, give me an advantage in my effort to rescue Ezra and Sarah..."

"You know I'll always help you, Kid. From—from beyond the grave, if I have to."

When she said this, her hands grew cold for a moment, and I felt a shadow creep across the room. It disappeared, it seemed, out the window, with the wind moaning just outside.

I didn't know what she meant, and I hesitated to ask. I loved Rosie for many reasons. She was my best friend's woman, and she'd correctly foreshadowed terrifying events in Virginia City that had prepared me for an air balloon battle above Ophir Hill and a showdown with French Confederates at the base of Mount Davidson. I was grateful to her, but I couldn't bring myself to learn if she'd used the stone to foresee her own death.

Because if she had, I'd be tempted to ask her to reveal my own demise.

Not that I believed in latter-day sorcery.

Warmth returning to her fingers, I pretended to concentrate. Instead, I observed, fascinated by the spell she cast over herself. Her eyes rolled back in her head, and her teeth began to clatter, the summoning of voices aging her appearance, wrinkles digging into her face. I'd seen it before, and it unnerved me. This time I was worried she might tell me something I didn't want to hear—namely that Ezra and Sarah had been tortured and killed by my father.

"He's here now," she said. "He laughs like a monster, Kid."

"He *is* a monster, Rosie. What is he saying?"

She took nearly a minute to respond, her brow furrowing and her mouth hanging open.

"I was wrong, Kid. Oh Lord, I was *so* wrong."

The hair on the back of my neck stood up. "Wrong about what, Rosie?"

"It wasn't your father speaking to me all this time. It's someone else."

"Who? Tell me, Rosie."

"He—Kid, he claims to be your brother. His name is—"

I released her hands and shot up from the table, chair loudly scraping the floor.

"Bartholomew. My older brother."

"He's been the one," Rosie said, "speaking to me this whole time."

Bartholomew was the son my father sired with his first wife, a woman named Mathilda, who died during childbirth. Bart grew up frail, his spine misshapen, his body a ruined thing. I recalled his handsome face, pale and aristocratic, like something out of a Velázquez painting. He'd played with me often, confined to a chair on wheels, a self-propelled, three-wheeled chassis that moved thanks to a system of cranks and cogwheels. My father had tasked one of his slaves with fashioning it based on an original design. Bart had played games with me whenever possible, teaching me the rudiments of chess, a game I later refined with the help of a tutor. I remembered his sadness, but I cherished my few memories of us together. I remembered how we explored the wildflower labyrinth, giggling as we hid from one another and the slaves who begged us to return to the house and eat lunch with my mother—his stepmother— the most beautiful woman we'd ever known. Bart was four years older than me, but he never condescended, never hurt my feelings. He always made time for me, even when exhausted by my father's incessant haranguing and daily training sessions.

Horse riding and target shooting were compulsory, my father hiring the best equestrians and marksmen to hone my brother's skills. Bart relished the attention for a while, but when the competitions grew more frequent so did my father's abuse. My brother routinely won first place at contests across the South, but if he stumbled—if he brought home a second-place ribbon or struggled to trounce a weak field of competitors—he received the lash. My father, perverse to his core, always watched, smiling eerily and with bated eyes, as a slave ripped Bart from his chair, bound him to a cotton-spinner, and dealt a whipping.

I'm sure Carson did much worse to his son, but it was something I never cared to ponder. Certainly not now. The longer I spent fiddling with apparitions in Rosie's apartment, the longer Ezra and Sarah remained in the clutches of Carson Crimson.

The spell broken, Rosie blinked her eyes, bringing her hands to her temple. "Before you broke contact with him, he told me a terrible secret."

"I know all of my brother's frightening secrets," I said. "I'm the one who found him dead."

My brother had blown his own head off with a hunting rifle to escape my father's endless wrath. I'd discovered his body in the library, a book splayed on his reading desk, Horace Walpole's *The Castle of Otranto*, the story of a prince obsessed with protecting his haunted castle. Searching for my mother, I crashed into her silk taffeta gown and wept tears of anger and relief. Bart had finally escaped my father, and yet I had no inkling of the hell into which Carson Crimson would plunge me, and of how he'd find a new quarry in my mother, killing her a few years later.

"Your brother urges you to avoid the narrow gorge," she explained. "Death waits for you there."

"There are lots of narrow gorges in and around Silver City," I said, rubbing my face with exasperation. "Devil's Gate is the first one we must travel to reach Silver City."

"Moonlight Canyon," she added, filling two water glasses for us to drink. "That's the one you're to stay away from."

I reached for the glass and examined it. The water quality in Virginia City was poor, but Rosie was scrupulous and boiled hers twice over. It looked good, so I downed it.

"Let's say you really did converse with my brother, Rosie. What did he say? Is he okay?"

She closed her eyes, shook her head. "He's in torment, Kid. He doesn't believe he'll find peace."

"I know the feeling," I said.

THE CARAVAN of stages nearly ready, I had to take care of one more item of business. I hurried to Roscoe's House of Hammers to procure a dozen gunpowder bombs wrapped in silver paper. Bringing any more than that risked, say, a trebuchet-launched fiery projectile striking the stage and igniting the fuses and any remaining Skorpion strength serum for a big send-off. I planned to rely on my buddy Snake's archery prowess to bring down the medieval weapons my father had directed at my Virginia City and my family.

When I arrived, Roscoe and his wife-to-be Emma had just sold their last shovel to the fire department in a hurry to bury the dead interlopers from Silver City, burned from Skorpion's flammable brew and eviscerated by shrapnel and mauled to death by Sarah's animal kingdom.

"Let me guess, Kid," Roscoe said. "You need more gunpowder."

Emma emerged from the backroom, and when she saw me, she touched her collarbone. "Kid, I heard the horrible news about the children. How can we help?"

"Give me a line of credit," I said, "on a batch of gunpowder tacos."

Roscoe had already reached into a barrel reserved for mining companies and was wrapping a bundle of twenty in a cotton blanket. "These are on the house. You're a good customer."

Emma reached for my arm, squeezing it. "Maybe our best. Bring them home safe, Kid. I—I miss riding with you like we did."

The shop door jangled, and I avoided looking at her fiancé. "That was fun. But this journey is significantly more dangerous."

"Running a gauntlet of trebuchets," Roscoe said, punctuating his statement with a whistle. "You're the only man who can save us from Armageddon."

I was about to ask for extra fuses when I saw their eyes focus on someone behind me. I heard the soft grunt of a wind-up and moved sideways along the counter, dodging the arc of a snooker rod.

Having missed with her forehand swing, Verbena,

eyes wild and teeth clenched, tried again with her back-hand. I got in too close for her to connect, shoved her into a stack of flour sacks while ripping the stick from her hands.

Then I snapped the cue against my thigh and tossed the fragments at her.

"Verbena," I said, tamping my anger. "I love you as much as my own mother. But if you ever again try to hit me with anything—even a feathered quill—I'll smack you like a soiled dove."

"Not surprising," she hissed, voice laced with venom. "It's how you treat all your women."

"What on earth do you mean, woman?"

"You let a disgusting magician disappear Ezra and Sarah, then abandon Poppy and your son so you can ride off with that repulsive writer from New York City. I should have Jericho and Chaparral horse whip you in front of the Assay Office for all to see!"

"I don't know how you can be more wrong with what you just spewed. I'm leaving with Jericho and Chaparral to rescue the kids, and I have no intention of leaving Poppy for my half sister."

This gave Verbena a slight pause. "She looks nothing like you," she said finally.

Emma came to my defense. "I can see it. In the eyes."

Verbena crossed her arms. "Shudder to think you're related to an East Coaster."

I pinched the bridge of my broken nose. "I'm riding into Devil's Gate, throwing myself and my friends into a crucible of trebuchets, and you're worried, on behalf of my wife, that I'm running away with a blood relative."

"Let's just say," Verbena said, "you're not the best communicator. And your morals have been known to be...dubious."

"Hang on," Emma said, coming around the counter to confront the saloon owner. "Kid is a gentleman who I've had the pleasure riding, and you should know that—"

"I bet you rode him," Verbena interrupted, capitalizing on Emma's gaffe.

"Darling," Roscoe said, wary of getting between them.

"Lord," I said. "I need to leave." But now, of course, I couldn't.

Shocked by Verbena's accusation, Emma opened her mouth, closed it with a furious expression, then threw a punch.

Verbena saw it coming, blocked it, and kicked the poor Mormon girl's shin.

"Ouch," she yelped, and then it was on.

Hair-pulling and hammer punching each other, they crashed into a display of iron pots, causing them both to topple over, with Emma ending up on top, delivering a flurry of punches, most of them striking Verbena's arms as she covered her face.

Roscoe ended the scuffle by yanking Emma to her feet and immediately swatting the dust from her dress. I, in turn, helped Verbena off the ground and spoke kindly to her.

"I know you're angry with me," I said. "I'm trying my best. Please let Poppy know that I'll bring Ezra and Sarah back to her unscathed."

"There's something you should know before you leave." Eyes glimmered like gemstones, her words put me on edge. I'd received too many revelations in the last twenty-four hours.

"If it's about my family, let's delay this information."

"It's about Devil's Gate," she said. "There's a secret secondary trail that only whiskey traders use. If you take that path, you can avoid the narrowest parts of the gorge. You'll still be ambushed, but you won't be ducks in a barrel."

She handed me a napkin from the Blood Nugget, the route drawn crudely in grease pencil.

"Verbena, I can't thank you enough."

She nodded. "I appreciate you, Kid. I didn't realize Clementine is your sister. And I'm sure you'd rather die than let anything happen to the Ezra and Sarah."

"Same goes for everyone here," Emma said.

Verbena gave them a somber look. "I'm sorry I reacted so poorly to Kid's assault on Silver City. I was upset, and I took it out on you, Emma."

Emma stepped forward and embraced Verbena, who returned the affection.

"We can't turn on each other," Roscoe said. "We should save our hostility for Silver City."

"Wish I could join you, Kid," Verbena said. "I'm not as good with a rifle as Poppy, but I can hit anything within fifty yards."

"Do me a favor."

"What's that?"

"Run and tell Poppy I love her."

"Deal," she said, kissing me on the lips. It was a prolonged gesture of affection.

I didn't resist as much as I should have.

20

I managed to catch Ralston on my way to the livery as he stepped inside the Dead Dice Saloon, Verbena's other establishment. I didn't have much time, but I needed to ask him a question.

I followed him inside the dimly lit bar, observing him sit at a table across from Sackmary, the gemologist who didn't know how to dig a hole in the ground. The two wore expressions as grim as the desert night.

Ralston's dark suit signaled wealth yet it was peppered with stains, suggesting he couldn't bother to finesse details. His frayed cuffs, too, indicated a life of anxious stock-market investments. He'd slicked his hair back meticulously, and his eyes, behind thin-rimmed spectacles, reflected the flickering light of an oil lamp. Sackmary, meanwhile, continued to project the aura of a spineless academic jellyfish. Somehow, he was still advising Ralston on financial matters.

Ralston saw me approaching and smiled...until he seemed to recall I'd nearly been pulverized by Molyneaux before a crowd of Silver City malefactors.

"Kid, have a seat," he said, snapping his fingers for a waiter to bring us whiskey.

"I can't," I said, still standing. "I'm off to Silver City. I need to know something—can I expect any help from Captain Connor and the Union army?"

Ralston sighed deeply. "The Indian problem has gotten worse, I'm afraid. On top of that, we've been getting reports all week about Silver City. The town is making serious inroads, and not just by thwarting stage-coach routes to California. There is active construction underway on a rail line into New Mexico Territory. We think your father is financing it."

I shook my head. "Glorieta Pass already decided New Mexico in favor of the Union."

Ralston took a draw from his cigar, smoke curling upward. His eyes, sharp and cold, met mine. "Union forces moved too far into Colorado Territory as Grant prepares the coup de grâce, so there's vulnerability now. What's worse is...well, Sackmary, why don't you explain it."

He looked weaker than the last time I saw him, and his voice sounded shaky from exhaustion. "Silver City has revealed a vein of silver bigger than anything we've seen on this side of the Comstock. Your father has already tapped into it, but according to my analyses—"

"That's really the problem," Ralston jumped in again. "Your father showed up and immediately got lucky. Silver City is offering better deals to miners, undercutting us at every turn. We've had to raise salaries to keep our men from leaving, and even then, we're hemorrhaging too much before the next quarterly report."

I leaned forward, my battered, bloody-knuckled hands on the table. "So I'm riding into Silver City without adequate support again, and you're telling me my father has stumbled into acquiring a huge deposit of silver?"

Ralston hesitated, looked at Sackmary and then me before lowering his voice. "We need you to handle it. We can't afford to wait for Captain Connor's return."

Sackmary's lips twitched into a wry smile. "You know your father's methods better than anyone, Kid. A few well-placed bullets are all that stands between saving Virginia City and watching your father's efforts curdle like old milk."

"Not just bullets," I said, my voice edged with anger. "My father is the devil incarnate, and he's already succeeded in kidnapping Ezra and Sarah. If they're not already dead, they're with him on the other side of Devil's Gate."

Ralston's eyes narrowed, a mix of calculation and manipulation dancing in their depths. He pulled a piece of paper from his suit, unfolded it, and slid it toward me. "I know, Kid, your line of work isn't fair or rational. But I want you to know I'm a man of my word."

I picked up the paper to read it. It was the deed to a piece of land, a grapefruit orchard in Sonoma County, California.

I could feel my eyes welling up with tears, knowing I held my long-nurtured dream in my hands, that all I had to do now was tear Ezra and Sarah from my father's evil grasp and whisk them away to the land of enchantment. My Poppy and my son Glade in a horse-drawn buggy, navigating rows of citrus, liberated from the stench of gunpowder and mercury and blood, free from the sight of people sacrificing themselves on the altar of other men's avarice and hunger for power. I was so close to victory I could taste it. I wanted to say thank you, but given that the children were in my father's sphere, I couldn't utter the words.

Seeing my reaction, Ralston's face brightened. "That property you have there isn't hanging over your head. You can walk away with it now, leaving Virginia City to burn, and enjoy your new life with Poppy and your son. Or you can stay one more day and undo your father's plans to eradicate the Union's silver, which finances the guns trained on your Southern kin."

I watched Ralston take another draw from his cigar, the embers glowing red in the dim light. Then I stood up straight and slipped the deed into my coat.

"You know I don't have a choice. I've grown awfully fond of the shoeshine boy and his Indian girlfriend. I'd rather die than leave them. I'd rather kill my father than leave him unpunished for one more minute."

Ralston nodded solemnly. "I understand. Your success is critical, and so is the safety of your children."

Sackmary coughed into his fist. "There's a gorge on the other side of Silver City you'll need to pay attention to."

"What gorge is that?"

"Moonlight Canyon."

Of course. "What about it?"

"It's where the vein is located. The one that threatens to enrich your father to an absurd degree."

"You want me to blow it up?"

The two men shared a look.

Ralston sipped his whiskey. "If you can't assassinate your father, we'll need you to bring down the walls."

"I can do that, but I prefer the former option."

"Thanks, Kid. We're building a new nation, and once the dust settles, it will be a glorious, united, and slavery-free land. Don't forget us when you reach California."

"I hope so, Ralston. And there's no chance of that." I tipped my gaucho and turned to leave.

The shadow of a doubt began to weigh heavily on my neck and shoulders. I left behind the rowdy dimness of the Blood Nugget, feeling the paper deed rustle in my coat and listening to the murmur of my friends harnessing their teams of horses as we prepared to lay siege to a neighboring town, my father having coiled himself like a viper in its heart.

———

WE FORMED a caravan of three Concord stagecoaches—Clementine, Hank, and I in the first wagon, Sam and Bad Jace in the second, with Larue bound in the carriage, and Chaparral and Jericho and Uncle John John in the third, with Uru secured in a cage on the wagon bed, hungry and snarling. Before setting out, I watched the animal yawn from nervous exhaustion after having bitten and maimed dozens of my father's men.

"Rest up, Uru," I said, tossing him a scrap of beef that John John had prepared for the beast prior to our mad dash through the canyon. "We'll need your strength in a few hours."

Kicking up a big dust cloud, we made our way toward Devil's Gate, determined to rescue Ezra and Sarah from the man who'd caused so much damage to me, a man who threatened to vanquish the future of Virginia City and Union efforts to win the War Between the States. I wasn't the only one who loved the children. Every man and woman with me—excepting Thurston Larue, of course—had affection for the mascots of the Comstock.

Hanging high in the bright sky, the sun cast a harsh, unforgiving light on the rugged canyon that carved a jagged path through the barren northern Nevada land-scape. Flanked by towering rock faces and craggy outcrops, the narrow pass reverberated with the thunder of hooves, the slapping of reins, and the cracking of whips—the nightmare cacophony of barely restrained violence seeking its target.

Three stages, wooden wheels spinning in blurs of motion, charged through the canyon. I watched Clementine straining against the reins as she fought to maintain control over the rearing horses. The ground beneath us was a tumultuous ocean of loose rocks and jagged stones. It felt like, at any moment, our stage would strike a rock big enough to smash our wheels and send us careening to our deaths. We moved relentlessly toward Silver City, guns in our hands and savagery in our hearts. We didn't relish bloodshed, but we were comfortable wielding it.

Ours was the lead coach, painted a gaudy yellow with red trim, rocking aggressively as we rumbled over a treacherous path. I gripped my seat, white-knuckling the rail with one hand while the other clutched a Winchester rifle.

The second coach followed close behind—perhaps *too* close—its paint chipped and faded, but its structure solid and determined. Bad Jace drove it like a bat flying from of the jaws of hell, while Sam, holding on for dear life, pinned his hand to the top of his derby, the wind and trail doing everything in their power to make him lose his hat.

The third coach, the most ominous of all, brought up the rear, its black iron plate-siding glinting in the sunlight, back end open to reveal a famished lion, lying on its stomach despite the rough ride, eager to cause more havoc if he wasn't soon reunited with his favorite human, the Paiute girl, Sarah. Chaparral was the least experienced driver among us, but he had nimble, fast-reacting hands, and I trusted him to make it through the canyon unscathed—mostly anyhow.

Above the din of our frantic journey, menacing shapes came into view—silhouetted beams of trebuchets being readied for their deadly task. Perched on either side of the canyon, massive weapons stood like ancient sentinels, their wooden frames reinforced with iron bands, their counterweights poised for destructive action. The sight of them was as foreboding as the storm clouds that accumulate and darken before a torrential downpour. Because we'd taken Verbena's whiskey trader route, we'd avoided certain death and had a chance now to survive the journey.

On the eastern ridge, the first trebuchet loomed, its operators working feverishly to prepare a volley of deci-mation for a part of the canyon they hadn't anticipated. These grim-faced men, clothes dusted with canyon silt, set fire to a kerosene-coated barrel filled with sand, creating a giant burning projectile for the sling. With a tethered, tension-releasing heave, the trebuchet's arm swung upward, the mechanism groaning under the strain. The barrel, glowing ominously, sailed through the air, black smoke and orange sparks trailing as it arced down toward us.

"Hold on, little brother!" Clementine said.

Blasting through the narrow pass, our stagecoach swerved as the fiery missile struck the canyon wall just ahead, sending a shower of rock and debris tumbling down. Eyes squinting against the dust and heat, the New York writer shouted over the roar of galloping horses, urging them onward as the coach lurched forward. Hank and I, sitting on either side of Clementine, clung desperately to anything we could grasp as we rattled and bounced over uneven ground. We were preparing to do something unusual to avoid getting bombarded.

The stagecoach behind us nearly slammed into the canyon wall as a cloud of dust obscured the treacherous path. The horses reared, breathing in frantic snorts as Bad Jace fought to steady the reins. The second trebuchet, stationed on the western ridge, had begun its preparation, the crew working with rehearsed efficiency, loading a fireball into the sling and adjusting its trajectory.

With a mighty heave, the trebuchet released its deadly cargo. A comet of flame and fury, the projectile crashed into the rocky ground just in front of the third coach, driven by Chaparral. The impact sent a shower of burning debris cascading over the path, forcing the driver to veer sharply to avoid the blaze. With the stage's armored exterior now soot-streaked and charred, Chaparral struggled to maintain speed as an inferno roared in his wake, Uru roaring, not in pain, but in fear of what more might come raining down on them.

The first trebuchet had reloaded and we were moving toward its best chance at smashing us. Careful not to lose our balance, Hank and I stepped out of the driver's seat to remove the hinge from the armored door of our stage. I planned to use it as a shield to deflect the oncoming missile. Hank used the claw of a hammer to rip out the pins, and soon I was carrying the door like a Greek shield, holding it by its handle. To his dismay, Hank accidentally ripped his hand open fumbling with the hammer.

"Ouch," Hank said, removing his shirt to wrap it around his hand.

"Stay down, Hank!"

He nodded and crawled under the passenger seats, bracing for impact. I reached the roof of the stage just as the fiery barrel came sweeping down to obliterate us.

Spotting a sniper in a rock cluster ahead, I pulled my pistol and took a shot. I missed the gunman, but hit the boulder next to him, the ricochet spinning the bullet into his hand. He dropped his rifle and, fingers crushed and bleeding, fell from his precipice into the dust forty feet below.

By this time, I turned to face the missile, using my improvised shield to deflect the barrel's trajectory and send it splintering and exploding into a pocket of pinyon trees, which went up in flames like dry tinder. The barrel had lost enough sand that when it struck the carriage door, it didn't have sufficient force with its glancing blow to knock me off the roof of the vehicle.

"You okay?" Clementine said, scanning me for burns.

"Never better," I said. "Don't stop until we reach the other side of hell!"

The ride was too bustling, so I stepped off the baggage, transferring the door back on its hinges so that Hank, seeing that the worst of the danger was over, could reinstall the door. Canyon walls closed in as we sped along, the air thick with the acrid odor of burning wood and scorched dirt, and mingling with the tang of human sweat and fear. Every impact of the trebuchet's projectiles produced tremors.

We drew near to the end of the pass, plunging through the narrowest section of the canyon where the walls seemed to press together. The horses' muscles bunched and rippled under their glossy coats as they strained against the reins, their eyes wide with fear. Clementine, with fierce resolve, lashed the horses forward, determined to get to the other side.

I looked behind us to see the second coach following in our perilous wake through a series of sharp turns and desperate maneuvers. Bad Jace, a veteran of dangerous routes, managed to keep the coach on course despite the chaos bubbling all around him. His eyes were fixed ahead, narrowing with every jarring bump.

The third coach, Chaparral's, was the last to clear the pass, nearly overwhelmed by the relentless assault from the trebuchets. Its armored exterior bore the brunt of the flaming barrels, but the driver remained stoic, unruffled, even as he pushed the horses to their limits.

One after the other, all three stagecoaches burst out of the narrow confines of Moonlight Canyon and into the wider expanse of the open desert. The trebuchets had missed their targets completely, the last few missiles sputtering out as they hit the ground far behind us.

My brother's ghost had warned me to avoid Moonlight Canyon, and now I knew why. There was no chance we'd make it through on the return trip.

If I didn't kill my father, I'd have to blow it up like Ralston suggested.

Dashing across the terrain, we saw Silver City straight ahead, the threat of trebuchets a fading memory. We are smoke choked but alive, and we exchanged relieved glances, our faces streaked with sweat and soot, guiding our weary teams toward the mining town less than a mile away.

"Now comes the real fight," I said.

Without a word, without looking at me, Clementine took one hand off the reins to grab my arm.

"I'm so happy I found you, Kid."

"You shared your feelings too soon, Clementine."

"No," she said. "I shared them before our father killed us both."

21

Silver City wasn't expecting a head-on assault. Believing the trebuchets were enough to thwart anyone daring to attack them with a full frontal, my father's ruffians focused on dragging mining equipment into Moonlight Canyon with mules and horses. They were gathered along the creek, watering their animals before putting them to work. When the men spotted our dust puff, they scattered instead of grabbing weapons to defend their town. And we soon found out that they had no snipers, either.

I had snipers in place, however.

Having left Virginia City before us, Bangs and Snake fired Whitworth rifles at the retreating men, bringing down a few. More important, my friends' gunfire stirred a panic, clearing the main road for us, so we could churn our way deeper into town and head right toward the Camel Hump, the saloon where I'd been reunited with my father.

No one confronted us in the streets, which was suspicious, unsettling.

"Are they really going to let us waltz right up to the saloon?" Clementine wondered aloud.

Hank struggled to hold a pistol with his bandaged mitt. "They're lying in wait."

He was right. We were coming down a small slope that led into the town's main business district when a Gatling gun cut loose from atop a water tower. Our horses were killed, the sound of their dying summoning the monster inside me. The three of us leaped from the driver's bench to take cover behind the carriage, splinters flying as the deafening weapon continued to throw screaming lead in our direction.

Driving the stage behind us, Bad Jace came over the rise and, seeing and hearing the carnage, smartly barked at his lead horse to move backward enough to use the slope as cover and avoid getting Gatling-shattered. He joined us, our backs to our beat-to-hell wagon, as the hand-cranked gun ran dry of bullets.

"That contraption talks louder than my first wife," Hank said.

"They're feeding it another ammo clip." Bad Jace handed me one Skorpion's explosive bottles. "Now's the time, Kid."

"I notice you're not rushing the tower yourself," I teased.

He laughed. "Someone's gotta stay behind."

"Don't die, Kid," Clementine said, her soft hand on my arm. "I didn't travel this far to see you gunned down."

I put her head in the crook of my arm and kissed her sweaty forehead. Then I got to my feet and ran toward the water tower.

The Gatling had just started to crank again when I tossed the Skorpion juice at the base of a column shoe and blasted it with my Colt. The detonation sent hot metal and fire slicing the air and ricocheting off a nearby drum of coal oil positioned next to a brick pile. The oil caught fire with a sudden whooshing sound, bursts of flame erupting from the containers. There was a screech as the support struts snapped and the riser pipe bent in half, the columns bending and breaking. The two men working the gun screamed as they careened from the platform they'd constructed atop the tower vent, hitting the ground with sickening thuds.

"We could use that gun!" I called over to Bad Jace.

"On it!" He and Sam leaped into action. I hoped they planned to install the Gatling on top of their as-yet-undamaged stagecoach.

Clementine was at my side, rifle in her hands as we marched toward the Hump. I kept my eyes on the roof, making sure no one planned to pick us off as we approached. At the same time, though, I had to register my surprise.

"You're different now," I said to my half sister. "The West has changed you."

"I'm glad for it," she said, spin-cocking her Winchester and stomping forward in her laced boots caked in mud.

They were waiting for us inside the saloon—my decadent father, at least a dozen thugs with guns holstered, but each carrying a club, and Tom Molyneaux the boxing champion, looking crispier than when I last saw him. He was breathing heavy, like a bull in a matador ring, flesh swollen and inflamed. His right hand, hanging uselessly at his side, was enlarged to a grotesque degree, his left wielded a sword, what seemed to be a Texas cavalry dragoon saber.

I couldn't help but ask, "How did you survive the flames, Molyneaux?"

"I have," he said, "an unusual tolerance for pain."

Carson Crimson laughed his wretched laugh. "The morphine helps, of course."

Molyneaux didn't respond to this, glaring at me with euphoric hatred instead.

"This is the end of Silver City," I said to my father. "Give me back the children so I don't do something you deeply regret."

"It's only the beginning, actually." His eyes burned with malevolence. "Don't worry, Kid. Ezra and Sarah are doing fine."

His overall demeanor was calm, even placid in his canary-yellow wool frock coat. It was what he used to wear while surveying his plantation on foot. Beneath the coat, he wore a crisp, white dress shirt with a high collar, a silk bolero, neatly knotted at his neck, adding a dash of refinement. His fitted wool trousers extended down into his boots, knee-high cut and practical for field inspections. A matching waistcoat complemented his coat and trousers, along with a broad-brimmed hat to shield himself from the sun. Once again, he carried that absurdly repugnant walking cane with the gold alligator head, a symbol of my devastated childhood.

"Where are they?" I was ready to raise my rifle and blow his head off.

"Safe in the box. Molyneaux, can you perform the honor?"

The boxing champion grunted, turning to retrieve Thurston Larue's chest, then using his boot to push it into the center of the room.

The careless way Molyneaux did all this enraged me, but I restrained my wrath.

At that moment, Bad Jace and the magician set foot inside, my fearsome friend having the sense to keep his barrel pointed at the ground.

"Looks like the man who can open the chest is here," my father said to them. "Please join us."

Larue hesitated, which irritated Bad Jace. Scowling, he shoved the magician toward the box.

"I've—I've never successfully completed a magic trick twelve hours later." He removed his dusty top hat to scratch his head.

"Open it now, Larue," I said. "Or I'll open *you* with a bullet." Then I addressed my father. "If they're hurt in any way, old man, you're as good as dead."

"I'm afraid," Carson Crimson said, "that's entirely up to your magician friend."

Larue closed his eyes, took a deep breath, and uttered his incantation, the same one he'd recited onstage in the Virginia City opera house. Then he took another step toward the chest, kneeled down, and touched both sides of the box.

There was the sound of a lock mechanism, and the lid slowly raised.

Blinking as if stirred from a dream, Ezra and Sarah slowly stood up in the box, side by side. Curiously, they held hands, like wax figures atop a wedding cake.

I pushed Larue aside, reaching for my adopted children, embracing them. To my horror, they didn't reciprocate, standing stock still, staring ahead blankly, obviously out of it.

I turned to give Larue a death stare.

"The stress of being hauled through Devil's Gate in a box," he said aloud, walking over to them, "was a lot to endure."

When I thought he planned to wake them from their

trance, he instead went past them to join my father on the other side of the room, smirking evilly.

"Larue," I hissed. "You bastard. Lincoln's favorite magician, huh?"

Larue reached for a bottle of whiskey that had been left on a nearby table. He popped the cork and took a swallow, wiping his mouth with his sleeve. "Spies walk among us everywhere. Some of us are better than others, as it happens."

My father seemed to have expected this outcome. He grinned, too, and with the help of one of his men stepped up onto a chair, then ascended to a tabletop. Pointing the tip of his cane at me, he watched the men surrounding him move toward us, clubs in their mitts.

"Your children are mine now, Kid. I'll raise them to serve the Confederacy. Something you were never willing to do."

"You murdered my mother, you bastard. You killed her and everyone else I ever loved."

"They were polluted, son. Polluted in the same way Lincoln and his race-mixing abolitionists want to see this once-great nation. It's time to create a new country, a vast circle of golden opportunity! It will require a bit of violence to realize a new world, naturally, but as you well know, son, I never skimp on violence. Neither do you, it seems."

The men drew closer, the fierce odor of their tobacco and sweat nauseating me. Clementine, Bad Jace, and I raised our rifles while retreating toward the batwings of the Hump.

"Don't leave, Kid!" Larue called out. "You haven't seen me perform my 'bullet catch' trick yet!"

As if on cue, Sam burst from the kitchen door adjacent to the bar, pushing the Gatling that now rested on a wheeled serving cart. Everyone turned, unsure about what they were seeing.

"Normally, I jest that we should leave guns to the low and unrefined," he said cryptically. "But in certain instances, the high-minded sophisticate must consent to have his soft hands dirtied."

Realizing what was coming, Clementine and I took the initiative to tackle Ezra and Sarah, respectively, knocking them flat on the floor and saving them from getting shot.

As if on cue, Sam cranked the gun, blasting from one end of the row of men to the other. It was splendid havoc, furniture chewed into smithereens and men riddled with bullets and poker cards fluttering like confetti into the air. I watched my father scramble down from the table and slide for cover beneath a roulette wheel, spinning after being grazed by a .50-caliber round.

Unfortunately, my friends were also in the line of fire and had to leap for safety to keep from getting grated like cheese by Sam's wild aim.

After what seemed like a full minute, the Gatling exhausted its bullets. The only man left standing was Larue, without a single peck of blood on his suit. He looked down, inspecting the length of himself for any damage and, finding none, smiled at Sam. At the same time, a bullet spilled wetly from his mouth, which he caught in his palm. He turned around to look at me, holding the bullet in the air like a trophy, beaming.

"Like I said, the bullet-catch trick!"

"Catch this." Bad Jace stood up to blast the magician with his Winchester.

Larue didn't. With an expression of terror, he gripped his chest, blood flowering his jacket. Then he fell over and died.

"I didn't know," Clementine said, brushing the dust from her jacket, "that Sam had it in him."

The groans of my father's dying men filled the air as Sam stepped over them to reach us. He was careful not to slip in gore, taking a moment, like a gentleman, to lay a handkerchief over the bullet-smashed face of one man.

"The children are safe," Sam said. "Our work is nearly done, and we can return to Virginia City now and watch the Union persevere and the American Dream unfold."

"Kid," Ezra said, his eyes vibrant again. "Where are we?"

"I'm hungry," Sarah said, holding her growling stomach.

"We're in Silver City, and I'll cook you both a steak as soon as we get back home."

A gunshot rang out, Bad Jace thrown back against a wall. Molyneaux then smashed the barrel of his flintlock against Sam's skull. Having lost our guns when we threw Ezra and Sarah to the ground, Clementine and I had nothing to return fire with. We raised our hands in surrender, along with the kids.

"You won't be returning to Virginia City," he said, "anytime soon."

22

GUN LEVELED AT US, OUR WRISTS ROPE-TIED behind our backs, the four of us—Clementine, Ezra, Sarah, and me—exited the saloon, Molyneaux prodding us toward a wagon hitched to two horses. My father took a moment to step up into the driver's seat, his age catching up to him and, I believed, the gunshot wound I'd given years ago had eroded his strength. He looked older, in other words, but no less dangerous. His venom remained lethal, and he still knew how to strike.

I had an inkling where he was taking us and hoped I was wrong.

"Up there on the ridge!" Carson Crimson shouted at Snake and Bangs, their silhouettes visible against the descending sun. "If you try to snipe us, I'll execute the children, Ezra and Sarah!"

My friends didn't respond, disappearing behind the ridge, so Molyneaux got into the wagon with us, flintlock at the ready.

"I'm begging one of you moves so I can shoot," he

said, gritting his teeth, finger on the trigger, eyes moist from the agony of his burns.

"Enough, Molyneaux," my father said, preparing a hypodermic syringe with what looked like an opium dose. "They're staying for dinner...but not much longer than that. Here you go, sir."

He reached behind the driver's seat to hand the boxer the morphine shot. Molyneaux jabbed it into the vein in his gun arm and pressed the plunger. His eyes grew heavier, but he didn't nod off like the men in Poppy's establishment. Instead, he wore a beatific smile.

"I'm happy now," he said. "And I'll be happier watching the four of you get eaten."

Ezra and Sarah looked at me, terror in their eyes. I gave them a confident head shake, letting them know there was no way they'd be hurt by this fool or anyone else.

"Molyneaux, last warning!" my father said. "A surprise is always the best, remember!"

"Yes, sir," Molyneaux said, drugged.

My father slapped the reins, and the horses slowly pulled us off the main avenue and down a path that led to a foundry powered by the nearby creek. Watching Carson Crimson maneuvering a wagon through town drew attention, men began following us on foot, a crowd growing before we arrived at our destination for a purpose known only to those who'd seen its horrors before.

"Don't worry," Clementine said to Ezra and Sarah. "Kid will get us out of this mess."

I nodded, clenching my jaw. My father was capable of anything, and I had a sinking feeling the spectacle about to unfold was anticipated by the onlookers gathering around us. Their faces displayed a mix of grim satisfaction and morbid curiosity.

"Step out," Molyneaux said, pushing the barrel of his gun into my chest. "Time for dinner."

Ezra closed his eyes and whimpered, snot pouring from his nose. As I got up to exit the wagon, he leaned into me with affection, a gesture that Molyneaux met with a wicked backhand.

"You'll get your turn, runt."

"Bastard," Clementine hissed.

Sarah looked at me stoically, but her anxiety was palpable.

My father remained in the driver's seat, looking at his handiwork. Beneath the wooden scaffolding was a swirling pit, a sulfuric hot springs, a shadowy form moving below the waters.

Molyneaux clocked me so hard in the face with his gunstock that I saw stars. Dizzy, I found myself at the edge of the platform, my wrists bound tightly with thick rope, coarse fibers cutting into my skin, beads of sweat on my face.

"I'll give you a hint. It's dog eat dog, eat or be eaten, survive or die," Molyneaux muttered into my ear.

I wound up to give him a body shove off the platform, but with a harsh creak, the trapdoor beneath my feet gave way. I fell, landing with a jarring splash into stagnant, warm, waist-high water. The pool was rank with rot. Darkness swallowed me momentarily. Struggling to find my balance, I made out the true nature of the hole.

It was an alligator pit.

The alligator, an enormous ten-footer with scales like ancient armor, lay coiled in the murk. Its eyes, cold and unfeeling, watched with a predatory gleam. The creature's jaws were lined with tusk-like teeth. Its powerful tail whipped through the water, thrashing a grotesque tattoo. The alligator's movements stirred the muck, the pit churning like an evil cauldron.

My first concern was to free myself from the ropes. The alligator's growl and hiss, the splash of its tail against the water, increased my desperation. I maneuvered my bound wrists against the rough, uneven walls of the pit, twisting and turning in an attempt to fray the ropes.

As the alligator's growl grew louder, closer, I redoubled my efforts, the rough stone of the pit working to my advantage. Gradually, the ropes started to fray. Now it was a race against time. With a final, determined twist, my hands were free.

Just then the alligator lunged with a sudden, violent motion, snapping dangerously close to my face. I rolled to the side, using a dead pinyon branch to smack the beast's maw and narrowly avoid a lethal bite. The pit's confined space forced the alligator and me into close quarters. My heart pounded, but my mind stayed focused.

Amid the debris, I spotted a large, jagged piece of metal. I seized it with such force that I cut my hand, but at least I had weapon. The alligator's tail whipped through the water again with tremendous force, sending debris into the air. I ducked and dodged, using the metal shard to strike the beast's snout, drawing hisses of pain.

It was a brutal dance of survival. The alligator's muscular tail made it difficult to approach, but I stayed just beyond reach.

With the beast growing agitated, I finally saw a chance. I noticed a length of rope that had fallen loose from my bindings. In a swift, decisive move, I grabbed the rope and managed to rodeo-loop it around the alligator's jaws. The creature thrashed violently, but the makeshift restraint partially subdued its mouth, reducing its ability to snap.

Seizing the opportunity, I slashed the softer underbelly, where the scales were thinner. Then I drove the shard into the vulnerable spots beneath the beast's jaws, the blade cutting through the hide, drawing streams of dark blood from both the gator and my hands that mixed with the murk of the pit.

The alligator roared and spun in agony, growing weaker with each thrust of the shard. The pit, once a place of my impending doom, was now a battlefield where my will to live was put to the ultimate test. With a final thrust, I shoved the sharp piece of metal far into the alligator's heart.

The beast convulsed one last time and then lay still, its massive body sinking into the muck. The water around it turned a dark, ominous red.

Exhausted, I stood over the defeated creature, my body smeared with grime and gore, my hands turned into pulp.

A rope was lowered to help me out. Hands mostly out of commission as the pain started to arrive, I wrapped the rope around my arms as best I could and hung on for dear life as I was pulled up. The harsh sunlight was a welcome relief after the darkness of the pit. The Silver City workers looked at me with awe and relief, their respect for me evident in their words.

"That was something else, young man," one said.

Another one whistled. "I've never seen an alligator this far west. And I've never seen one bested by a man with his wrists tied."

"I'm from the swamp," I said, "where we eat gators for breakfast."

I looked around but didn't see my father or scarred-up Molyneaux or the wagon containing my family.

"Where are they?" I said, blinking insanely from the muck in my eyes. I grabbed one of the workers by his collar. "Where did they go!"

"Moonlight Canyon," the spectator said. "Where silver ore shines in the night like fallen stars."

"I'm throwing a curtain over those stars," I said.

A wagon came roaring up to the platform and pit and I was never so happy to see Bad Jace in my life. He climbed down from the driver's seat in obvious pain and stumbled onto the platform, clutching his bloody, bullet-nicked shoulder.

With him was Sam, rubbing his head after the crack Molyneaux had given him. "The three of us are a mess. But my need for vengeance is piqued."

Bad Jace raised a pistol at the man who'd answered my question. "Bring us three horses. Now."

"You can put the gun down, the man said, unimpressed. "We're not fighting you." He nodded at his friend, who scampered over to the post where several horses were chewing hay. "I guess I should've known if you could kill the Annihilators, then lassoing a gator wouldn't be much trouble."

I recognized the voice. My vision was clearing, the man was starting to look familiar. "Gentry! Hank and I found you at Cisco."

He showed me some clean rags, saying, "We need to get those." As he worked his way around my tattered flesh, he said, "You sent us to Fort Churchill, but we ended up in Silver City. The money being offered was too good. The Annihilators made sure we earned it and then some. That is, until you took them out."

Bad Jace lowered his gun, realizing I was with acquaintances. "Kid is good at wasting vermin."

Bringing over two horses, Joaquin, the other man I'd encountered at Cisco who had been determined to box me, was impressed by my gator wrestling. "I owe you an apology, Kid. You're cleaning up this town like you did Virginia City. I had you pegged wrong."

"No apology needed," I said. "Gentry, you should know your brother Buzzard is mining in Virginia City. He saved my life, and he's worried about you. If I survive this ordeal, come on up and visit him. I'll buy you both a round of whiskey."

"You'll survive," Gentry said. "Me and Joaquin and many more of us are joining you and your friends. Your father is an insane bastard and needs to be stopped. What he's done to some of the women here, the saloon girls in the saloon...well, it's just unspeakable evil is what it is. On top of that, our paychecks are late."

"Grab a gun, then," Bad Jace said, laughing. "No more talking. Let's stop Carson Crimson from ripping more money out of Moonlight Canyon. His hunger for power won't end unless we end him."

"It will take everything we have," I said. "How's Uru doing on the wagon?"

"She's quite famished," Sam said. "Otherwise, beautiful."

Bad Jace's shoulder wound caused him to wince. "I say we feed her."

It didn't take long for us to saddle up and head toward the gorge. I drove the wagon with Uru in his cage and could almost hear his stomach rumbling from hunger pangs over the noise of the carriage wheels. When I unlocked the cage, if given the chance, what fury might Uru inflict? I had to admit I was curious. I was curious about a lot of other things, too—like how I'd ultimately kill my father. I'd harbored a lot of fantasies, but the most satisfying one involved strangling him to death with my bare hands and watching the light fade from his sinister eyes.

Not every man who rode with us had a gun, but they all seemed eager to take on Carson Crimson and his thugs, and there were plenty of knives and shovels to go around. We were a haggard bunch, Gentry and Joaquin having come off a brutal thirty-two-hour mining shift and no sleep. Still, they seemed in pretty good spirits as we drew closer to the gorge.

"How are we going to do this?" I asked Gentry, riding a draft horse alongside the wagon.

"We'll drop into the shaft and pop out of another access point deeper in the canyon."

"What do you think he plans to do with my family?"

Gentry looked at Joaquin, mounted on another draft. I could tell they didn't want to tell me.

But Joaquin said finally, "Your father is dragging them inside the Cavern of Dreams."

"What's that?"

"It's where the poison vapors are strong and give men visions."

Bad Jace spat his chaw into the dust. "Why bring Kid's family there?"

"A nugget the size of a human skull is lodged in the cavern. Carson has been talking for days about finding a child small enough to pry it loose."

I felt my heart beating in my chest. "He couldn't find one in Silver City to dislodge the deposit?"

"The children of this town," Gentry said, defeat in his eyes, "had all disappeared long before he found the silver."

23

WE ANGLED OUR HORSES AND WAGON DOWN the bend in the trail leading to the deepest part of the gorge, where the mouth of a cavern yawned open. The plan was for me and Gentry to pick our way through the tunnels until we reached the spot where the silver nugget was located and rescued the children and Clementine. Gentry had been among the first group of miners to discover the deposit, so he knew better than anyone how to reach the part of mine that Carson Crimson didn't know about. A break in the wall had developed over time and with a solid push we could reach the deposit. The others—Bad Jace, Sam, Joaquin, along with Snake and Bangs—would grab Molyneaux and my father and wait for us to emerge.

"I rarely spend time in the mines," I said, bandanna over my face to help me deal with vapor. "All my assignments have been aboveground."

"Getting cold feet?" Bad Jace said. "Or did the alligator wear you down?"

Everything had me worn down, from long before the

fight with the big reptile. But since then, I couldn't stop trembling from utter exhaustion. I had to hold on a little longer though, and save my family from the menace of Carson Crimson.

"I'm not scared of being interred. I've been preparing for it my whole life."

"There was a gemologist from Virginia City who visited our town quite a few times and seemed to know a lot about you," Joaquin said casually. "He mentioned you sleeping in a coffin in an undertaker's office for years before you married an opium nymph."

This bit of information stopped me in my tracks. "Does his name happen to be Sackmary?"

Joaquin furrowed his brow. "Yes, that's him. He met with your father regularly. He seemed very excited about the discovery of the nugget."

"He's the one," I said to Bad Jace, "who told my father about Ezra and Sarah. That's why my father took them from me."

"You're taking them back," he replied, handing me a gunpowder taco. "They belong to you and Poppy and Virginia City."

With a final nod to Bad Jace, I descended into the mine with Gentry leading the way. We both carried oil lamps that illuminated the underground cavern. The air was thick with dust, and the farther we went, the more oppressive the darkness became. The mine's tunnels were a labyrinth, twisting and turning with each step. I'd navigated tunnels before, but never under such dire circumstances. The usual hum of mining activity was replaced by an eerie silence, broken only by the occasional drip of water from the ceiling.

The fumes were already getting to me, and I told Gentry as much.

"We need to get closer to the ventilation holes," he said. "If we don't, we'll suffocate."

After what felt like an hour, we reached a fork in the tunnel. I had no way of knowing which path led to my abducted family. Gentry seemed confused too. He paused, closing his eyes.

Together, we listened. Distant cries and the clanking of metal on rock were faint, but unmistakable. We looked at each other, and with renewed determination we took the left path, our boots crunching loose gravel.

As we made our way deeper into the mine, the passage became narrower, the walls closing in on us. With the oppressive heat, it was hard to breathe and sweat riveted from our brows. I wiped my face with the sleeve of my coat and pushed on. Now the cries grew louder, more frantic, along with the metallic sound.

My heart pounded in my chest, but I forced myself to stay calm.

Gentry spoke quietly. "Sounds like one of them might be stuck inside the cavern."

I listened again. "That's Ezra. Let's get him out of there."

Eventually, we rounded a corner and came upon the wreckage. This part of the tunnel had collapsed, leaving a heap of rocks and debris blocking the way. But we could see through to the other side and the tight drop where Ezra was stuck, his leg wedged between the cavern wall and the watermelon-sized nugget that he'd been forced to remove.

In the dim light of our lanterns, I could make out the outline of the boy. As we drew closer, I pushed Gentry aside and saw Ezra's face, pale with fear. His eyes went wide when he spotted me.

I brought my finger to my lips, and he obeyed.

"Sarah and Clementine?" I whispered, yanking away my bandanna.

He pointed upward and in a hushed tone said, "Outside the mine. In the wagon."

"Have you chipped it loose, boy?" It was my father's voice, booming from above the borehole opening.

I indicated he should respond.

"Y—yes, sir," Ezra said. "I chiseled it free."

In a moment, the knotted end of a rope dropped down.

"Tie it around the silver rock," my father instructed. "Hurry now. Your sister is hungry."

"Yes, sir."

I handed him a useless rock to tether. He succeeded with, of all things, a timber knot, wrapping the rope around the stone. I handed the silver nugget to Gentry, eyes wide with the promise of treasure.

"My goodness," he whispered.

I wedged a gunpowder taco beneath coarse fiber as a little surprise for my father and Molyneaux.

"It's coming up now, sir."

As the stone began to rise, I struck a match against a rock and lit the fuse.

Then I pulled Ezra through the opening and the three of us scrambled back through the tunnel that brought us to this spot, hoping not to get crushed in a cave-in.

"Kid!" Ezra cried, slowing ahead of us.

"Keep moving!" Gentry said. "It's gonna be—"

A loud explosion shook the walls, blasting us with a gust of air that sent us flying face-first onto the graveled cavern floor.

Choking on dust, I looked around and saw my lantern barely glimmering in the darkness. I picked it up, but all I saw was fluttering silt.

"Ezra? Gentry?"

I started digging frantically through the debris. The weight of the rocks and the creeping dread that I might not reach them in time were overwhelming. Sweat stung my eyes, my muscles screamed in protest, but I couldn't stop. To my relief, I found a small pocket in the wreckage and managed to pull Ezra by his limp shoulders halfway out from under a pile of rocks.

"Thank God," I said, though I wasn't sure if I believed what was happening. "Now breathe!"

Ezra coughed. "My legs are stuck."

With a final, powerful heave, I pushed a large boulder aside to create a gap just wide enough for him to crawl through. I pulled him into a tight embrace, his eyes brimming with tears.

"We're not out yet," I said, my voice a fierce whisper. "We have to get Sarah and Clementine."

Gentry groaned, emerging from the rubble like a buried corpse, silt waterfalling off his body.

"I'm all turned around," I said. "Can you get us out of here?"

He sputtered dust before answering. "Yes."

We made our way back through the mine, Gentry leading and holding the lantern high. The journey back seemed to take forever, the air growing heavier, less breathable, with each step.

Finally, after what felt like an eternity, we emerged from the darkness and into the fading light of the evening.

I clapped Gentry on the back. "You did it. You got us in and brought us back, Ezra with us."

Gentry's dust-covered face cracked into a smile. "Just did what I had to." Then he checked to see that the nugget had arrived with us too.

As the sun set over Silver City, a cool breeze brought relief. Stars twinkled in the vast expanse above. Ezra was safe, and with any luck my gunpowder bomb had taken out my father and his henchman. There was a strange scent on the wind, however.

"Let's move around to the main access," Gentry said, "and see if Joaquin and the others secured the women."

"I'd say that's a no." Standing on the outcropping above was Molyneaux, gun pointed at us.

———

USING his cane to help scale the rocky incline and breathing heavily from the effort, my father joined his enforcer. To my amazement and horror, and I'm sure to Ezra and Gentry's, Carson Crimson had with him, collared and leashed, another alligator, this one even bigger than the one I'd stabbed in the murky grotto. My father smirked as he looked down at us, an expression— and an angle—I was all too familiar with as a child. It made me sick to my stomach to see him gloating above me.

"You had some help finding the boy," he said. "You were always very accomplished, Kid, at making new friends. Even in the boxing pits of Macon."

"That might be the first compliment you ever paid me, you sick son of a bitch."

"There will come a time, son, when the world you see around you resembles an ocean of misery and toil and bloodshed. You will huddle with your family in the earliest part of the ordeal, but then the realization will settle in your mind—you'll need to take things from people, people you once called your friends, for you and your family to survive. And when you secure what you need, when you rip what you want from the fingers of the damned and the lost and the unprepared, you will finally, son, in that moment of triumph, thank me."

"So this is all an ongoing lesson, a prolonged test?" I said, my heart bleeding out in front of Ezra. "Throwing me into an alligator pit? Stealing my family? Killing everyone in Virginia City?"

He chuckled darkly. "Honestly, no. I take pleasure in molding you. And I take pleasure in remaking the world."

"You're a crazed raving bedlamite who the world will be much better off without."

"Perhaps. It doesn't matter, really. But remember your Romans, son: *Not only so, but we also rejoice in our sufferings...*"

"*Because we know that suffering produces perseverance,*" I said, completing the verse. "*Perseverance, character. And character, hope.*"

"In a way, son. I've instilled in you a great sense of hope."

"The only thing I hope for is your slow violent agonizing death."

Ezra took my hand in his, seeming as if he was waiting, like me, for Molyneaux to shoot us down.

"I tried my best with you," my father sighed, reaching down to unfasten the leash on his pet swamp lizard. "Sometimes an investor must abandon a project out of necessity. Most people believe in the fallacy of sunk costs, you know. They tend to continue with an endeavor they've invested money, effort, or time into. Even as the continued expenses outweigh the benefits. An investor, however, sees it differently. A smart, successful investor drops the curtain."

Freed from its tether, the beast, eager to take a bite

out of us, crawled like a primeval horror down the small escarpment, pebbles and stones clattering at our feet.

Gentry turned and ran but didn't get far. Molyneaux's gun boomed, and my miner friend went down hard, collapsing against a scrub bush, splattering it with his blood.

"Kid," Ezra said, legs trembling. "I don't want to be eaten by a dinosaur."

"Stay behind me," I said. "I've already killed one of these monstrosities. I can kill another."

I tried to pick up a big enough rock to bash the alligator's brains in, but my hands were completely shredded from my first wrestling match in the grotto and digging Ezra and Gentry out of the rubble.

Ezra and I were too high up the mountain to jump anywhere that wouldn't shatter our legs.

With an almost unearthly clarity, I saw my father's final checkmate. I had three moves, one more terrible and pointless than the next. Fling Ezra and myself to our certain deaths, get ripped apart by a creature from my worst nightmare, or run to get shot in the back.

I was far beyond the point where I could decide and waited for what happened first—and last.

What happened was Uru the lion leaped from a lower part of the spur with a roar, landing on the alligator's spine, digging his incisors into the upper half of the creature's snout and tearing.

Hissing like a dragon, the alligator spasm-flipped, trying to shake loose the jungle cat that had suddenly pounced. The two mighty creatures clashed like a blood-curdling dream.

I clutched Ezra and took him to the ground underneath me to protect him from the rifle shot I knew was seconds away, but amidst the din of battle, I heard a roar, this one from a human. I looked up to see Molyneaux's face contorted with pain, yelling profanities, from being shot through the back of his arm, the one leveling the gun, with an arrow. Without hesitation, he used his other arm to pull the arrow all the way through, screaming as blood poured from the wound.

But then he smiled as he held up the dripping arrow.

The mirth disappeared as he watched Carson Crimson cane-hobbling away as fast as his rickety legs could carry him, always at least a step or two ahead of risk to himself. That turned out to be another arrow, this one landing at Molyneaux's feet, fuse hissing along the bolt. The boxer switched the flintlock to his good arm and swiveled the barrel to point it at the mysterious archer.

"Hold on tight!" I shouted at Ezra.

The explosion nearly knocked us right off the mountain. I managed to grab the roots of a mining-ravaged pinyon tree to keep us both from plummeting into the abyss.

I pinned the boy to the edge of the cliff as a landslide engulfed us, rocks battering my spine like fists, the mountain rumbling like an earthquake. Somehow, I succeeded in shielding Ezra from the worst of the onslaught. Silt choked the air, our surroundings obscured in a suffocating haze. Teeth still gritted, I waited for more debris.

As the avalanche subsided, the dust began to settle. Miraculously, we were relatively unharmed, Ezra cradled in my arms, safe from the lunatic violence of my father and his vicious sidekick.

We both took ragged breaths and when I inspected him for injuries, I saw his eyes, though weary, glinting with determination.

"I knew you could do it, Kid." He hugged me harder than I'd ever been held.

In the silence that followed, our gratitude and relief mingled with the echo of crunching footsteps. Bad Jace, Snake, Bangs, and Joaquin arrived, looking down at us with concern. Snake was armed with a bow, quiver of arrows at his back.

Clementine and Sarah, both smiling and with tears in their eyes, walked to the precipice, my worries allayed.

"Everyone cleared out after the second explosion," Bad Jace said. "You packed a lot of punch in those tacos, Kid."

Someone emitted a groan behind me. I saw Gentry moving amidst the debris, in obvious pain. Bleeding from a wound in his left hip from Molyneaux's gunshot, he was still alive.

Bad Jace and Snake picked up fallen pine branches, taking small steps as they descended the outcropping to reach us. Only through sheer grit and willpower did I hold on to the largest limb as we were pulled up, my hands sliced up as they were, until Snake grabbed my collar and yanked me off the cliff. Bad Jace was already trying to help Gentry, spitting dust from his silt-plastered mouth, to his feet. Gentry waved him away, then limped back to the spot where he'd fallen to retrieve something.

It was the bucket-sized nugget of silver my father had tried to pull from the canyon.

Smiling, ignoring the seeping wound in his side, Gentry cradled the jagged deposit in his arms like a tender infant. "I don't care if I have to split this ten ways. Look at the size!"

When Ezra and I were safe on the mountain, Clementine and Sarah were there, eager to hug us. We hugged them right back, the four of us reunited.

"I have news for you little ones," I said.

"Sorry," Clementine said, scrunching up her face into a don't-be-mad-at-me mask.

"You told them already?"

"I was too excited."

Sarah rubbed her hands together theatrically. "I'm so glad it's a boy. Now I can teach him how to ride horses and shoot at the same time."

"I'm going to call him Bad Glade," Ezra said.

I tousled Ezra's grimy hair, my heart swelling with the knowledge that both my first-born and the deed to my land were in Poppy's safekeeping. The smoking ruin of Molyneaux's corpse brought me back to reality.

We searched the canyon until Snake found the tracks of expensive boots, but they disappeared into the scrub that ran along the end of the lower ridge. A shattered walking stick, the bottom half of the golden gator-headed cane, was lodged in the padded limbs of a prickly pear. A windstorm picked up, and the trail vanished.

Once again, the crafty old bastard denied me the satisfaction.

24

I'D POSITIONED EZRA TO MONITOR THE ASSAY office up on B Street and report to me as soon as what I'd suspected, and now knew to be true, happened. I didn't think it would take long and it didn't.

At home, recovering from my various wounds and infirmities and enjoying time with Poppy and Glade, on the third day Ezra burst in through the side door and exclaimed, "Kid! He's here! Just like you said!"

I was ready. I stepped out onto A Street and strode down the hill a block to see a gemologist with a reputation for financial meticulousness, clad in a well-worn, charcoal-gray suit that hinted at East Coast status, step out of a rickety horse-drawn carriage. His polished leather boots crunched on the gravel of B Street as he made his way to the Assay Office, an unassuming structure with a faded sign swinging gently in the arid breeze.

I followed him inside. Shafts of sunlight pierced the dusty window, the air thick with the smell of metal, stone, and ink.

His gaze swept over rows of shelves lined with vials

and scales before settling on the sturdy wooden counter, where a grizzled clerk with a face like crumpled leather sat scribbling notes.

"Mr. Sackmary, I presume?" the clerk greeted him without looking up.

The gemologist nodded, stepping up to the counter and produced a set of documents. "I'm here to secure the mining claim I mentioned before," he said, voice high-pitched yet steady, fingers drumming lightly on the counter.

The clerk reached for the papers. As he did, the creak of the floorboard behind him drew Sackmary's attention.

I wore a wide-brimmed hat that shadowed my face and a black coat that swallowed the light.

Sackmary's eyes narrowed slightly as he struggled to recognize me. When he finally did, his eyes widened.

"Evening, Kid," he said with strained politeness, trying to maintain his composure.

I said nothing, staring at him.

The clerk looked up, clearly uneasy as he sensed a brewing confrontation. Sackmary's fingers tightened around the edges of his documents.

This time, he stammered when he spoke. "K—Kid, I assure you, the claim is entirely legal. I've followed every regulation and rule."

My hand hovered casually near my hip, then my fingers came to rest on the handle of my Colt.

"You were working with my father the whole time," I said. "Maybe even before you arrived."

He looked at the clerk for support and received none. "I'm merely here to file a claim. If you have any disputes, they're best handled through proper channels. We're in a civilized town."

"I'm the one who civilized it," I said. "You're the one

who tried to tear it down, with the help of my father. Tear it down and hand it over to the Golden Circle."

Sensing the escalating danger, the clerk cleared his throat. "Mr. Crimson, you'd best take your grievances up with the Land Office instead of disrupting the proceedings here."

I looked at the clerk. "He'll need to sign a few documents."

"More than a few," the clerk harrumphed. "Mr. Sackmary is seeking a claim on the edge of Moonlight Canyon outside Silver City. All of this information will be posted in tomorrow's Territorial-Enterprise. Aboveboard and transparent, Kid."

I turned my attention back to Sackmary. "Right-handed?"

"Excuse me?"

"Are you right-handed, Sackmary?"

He swallowed. "Left. Left-handed, actually."

"Let me see."

Confused and sweating now, he slowly raised his left hand.

I took a pen from my jacket and pushed it into his palm, forcing him to grasp it. Then I placed a set of documents on the counter between Sackmary and the clerk.

"Ralston prepared these with the help of the Assay Office in Silver City," I said. "You're applying for and purchasing the claim, then have it transferred to a trust for the benefit of the Lydia Sweet School of the Fourth Ward of Virginia City, Nevada."

"Kid," Sackmary said. "That claim is worth millions. I can't—"

"If you want to leave here," I interrupted, "with the use of all your limbs, you'll do what I say."

He nodded, eyes welling with tears, turning toward the counter to begin signing papers.

"Now, Kid," the clerk said, "this is highly inappropriate."

"I'm sure. But you're not going to mention it to anyone."

He said nothing for a moment. "Kid, what on earth did this gemologist do to you?"

"He tried to feed me and my family to alligators in a fetid pond of mining waste."

"Alligator? In Nevada? I've never heard of such a thing, but I have no reason to doubt it. If it's as you say," the clerk intoned, authorizing each page after Sackmary had signed it, "I guess that would rightfully enrage a person."

———

INDIAN SUMMER in Virginia City was especially dreamlike that year. As ugly as the town grew, with an increasing number of mining operations underway and the unsavoriness of the population changing to Sackmary's ilk from Bad Jace's, Poppy, the children, and I savored every minute of our time spent there. Ezra shined the shoes of visiting politicians. Sarah taught Uru how to nap in the Sure Cure without mauling any of the customers. And my flower, my loveliest Poppy, cared for our son Everglade and cherished him thoroughly, effortlessly. Grover took time out from rebuilding his mortuary to shoot photos of the mother and her newborn, and even built a crib for Everglade to sleep in.

After learning her husband had been killed in the war, Clementine founded her own newspaper, a competitor to

Sam's *Territorial Enterprise*. They continued their writers' dance, both in public and private, but both knew its days were numbered, and Sam eventually disappeared after changing his name to avoid gambling debts. He ended up one of the most famous people in the world, around which he traveled at least twice, surprising none of us. He also went bankrupt not once, but twice, by making investments in harebrained inventions, which surprised all of us. I loved him for who he was and how often he pulled me out of danger when the chips were down. A better friend I never met.

Clementine continued to write her penny dreadfuls about a Kid Crimson that no one, least of all me, recognized, but the more fictionalized she made them, the better they sold. She started spending more and more time with Grover and the last I heard, he was building a big new house on A Street, though he was coy when I inquired about its size.

Verbena expanded her saloon empire to Silver City.

Before becoming a famous New York composer, Chaparral finally got to premiere his symphony at the opera house, relying on a crackerjack cadre of musicians that Ralston shipped over on stagecoaches, one of them driven by Hank Monk. He took Rosie with him to New York and she made a fine living as a fortune teller at Coney Island—when she wasn't caring for the brood that the two of them produced.

Hank died after a spill on the route, but his legacy lived on. Like Grover, he was like a father to me and I grieve his loss to this day.

Jericho ended up running a small bar of his own, the Double Shot, and working again as a firefighter, a job that had previously unraveled his nerves. But after spending so much time fighting violent and gunpowder-laden Confederate conspiracies with me, he realized dowsing a burning structure with water wasn't all that intimidating an occupation after all.

To keep Lydia happy, Bad Jace shaved his beard, cut his hair, bathed regularly, and helped her at the school, which eventually grew to four stories and hundreds of children, when he wasn't maintaining order in town after being appointed Virginia City's first sheriff with Ralston's backing.

Ralston moved to San Francisco where he founded the Bank of California. He built himself a nice mansion on Nob Hill, spent five million on the opulent Palace Hotel, and was involved in a diamond-investment hoax. He was wiped out by the Crash of '73 and was found in San Francisco Bay soon thereafter. Whether he had a stroke or committed suicide was never determined.

The silver nugget was assessed at just over a million dollars. Gentry and Joaquin took their share and, with Gentry's brother Buzzard, invested in a piece of railroad technology that made them all wealthy, though not happy. Each of them struggled with the bottle and didn't end up with any children or grandchildren to whom they could pass along their riches.

I never heard from or about my father again. He simply disappeared off the face of the earth as he fled from the gunpowder taco that Snake shot at Molyneaux's feet. I like to think he finally got what was coming to him, though I don't think about him much anymore.

The Civil War ended, but some of the old antagonisms still had momentum that Bad Jace, as a law enforcer, had to contend with, putting aside his own sympathies. But as the mines started to play out and the transcontinental railroad was built, creating Reno, Truckee Meadows was in ascendance, while Virginia City started to decline. Then the Big Fire of 1872 destroyed most of the town, which was half-heartedly rebuilt. Then it faded slowly, like a dream.

The Crimsons left for the sunny climate and verdant foliage of California and never looked back. Sarah became known as an otherworldly veterinarian, given her abilities with creatures of all kinds, sizes, and infirmities. Ezra, enterprising lad that he was, carved out some seemingly useless acreage in the back forty of the orchard to grow a variety of cash fruits that weren't well known in California but became popular: cherries, nectarines, plums. He even discovered and experimented with avocados, developing a cold weather variety that survived the occasional frost. Poppy birthed me three more sons and launched a chain of flower shops in Sonoma County that served weddings, christenings, and holiday. Verbena and Jericho got married and moved their operation to Reno, as did a number of other businesses, further depressing the old boomtown. Clementine eventually moved here too. Our family took the train up to Reno once or twice a year from Oakland to visit Poppy's family.

The orchard business was tough, but I had the best partner in Snake. He and his girlfriend Estrella, who finally warmed up to me in California, were terrific gardeners and saved my yields from deep freezes and wildfires. Sometimes we reminisced about killing bastards in northern Nevada over whiskey, but as we grew older, we understood that that was a young man's game better left to younger men.

There was the time, however, when Glade got into trouble in Santa Rosa for walking with a Mexican girl in broad daylight, the brazenness of which upset farmers on one side and pickers on the other. It was an incident that required Snake's and my intervention.

I'll tell you about it one day soon. Right now, there are grapefruits ripe for picking.

ABOUT THE AUTHOR

Jarret Keene is an assistant professor in the Department of English at UNLV, where he teaches American literature and the graphic novel. He is the series editor for Las Vegas Writes, published by Huntington Press, and is the author of *Hammer of the Dogs*, and the middle grade books *Decide and Survive: The Attack on Pearl Harbor* and *Heroes of World War II: 25 True Stories of Unsung Heroes Who Fought for Freedom*. Keene has been interviewed by *Writer's Digest*, *Publisher's Weekly*, *EcoTheo Review*, *Library Thing*, *Black Fox Literary Magazine*, and Coast to Coast AM.